MOONLIT SECRETS

A Harry Sinclair Cozy Travel Mystery: Book 2

Sabina O.

CORTIJO BERRUGUILLA

For permission requests, write to:

Sabina Ostrowska, penname Sabina O.

textworkshop.org

Cortijo Berruguilla

18270 Montefrio

Spain

sabina.a.ostrowska@gmail.com

First Edition

ISBN: 978-84-09-67086-4 (paperback edition)

ASIN: B0CW1JQD2H (e-book edition)

ALSO BY

A Harry Sinclair Cozy Travel Mystery series so far:

Shadows of Serenity

Moonlit Secrets

Whispers of Lotus Villa

Sabina's Humorous Non-fiction Series:

The Crinkle Crankle Wall: Our First Year in Andalusia

A Hoopoe on the Nispero Tree: Our Andalusian Adventure Continues

Olive Leaf Tea: Time to Settle

CONTENTS

PROLOGUE

The woman woke to the sound of rumbling outboard engines and the acrid smell of salt water mixed with gasoline. Confused and disoriented, she squinted into the dark, trying to make sense of her surroundings. As her eyes adjusted, she realized she was lying on a rough couch inside the cabin of a small motorboat. The cool sea air clung to her skin like a moist veil.

Slowly, she sat up and looked around. Across from her, two Thai women sat quietly, tired and absorbed in their thoughts. They were dressed in party clothes: sequined tops, short skirts, and gaudy makeup that was now slightly smudged. She felt a knot tighten in her stomach. What had happened? Where was she? A panicked thought flashed across her mind: *Where is everybody?*

The woman opened her mouth to ask what was going on but then decided to remain silent. Something wasn't right. She looked to the right and saw two older Thai men—one by the boat's engine and another at the boat's wheel. One of the men seemed vaguely familiar, but she couldn't place him; her dull head was pounding, preventing her from thinking clearly.

She glanced out into the inky darkness of the ocean. Other than the narrow beam of the boat's headlight, the world around her was pitch black. Her heart thumped loudly against her ribcage as a terrible sense of dread washed over her.

Who are these people? And where are they taking me?

The boat cut swiftly through the water, its destination as murky as the thoughts clouding her mind. Her instincts screamed that something was profoundly wrong, but her throbbing headache and dizziness made it impossible to think straight.

CHAPTER 1

ON THE FERRY

The passengers from Koh Samui to Koh Phangan comprised an eclectic collection of souls. Thai locals sat alongside sunburnt tourists, who buried their faces in guidebooks or gazed in wonder across the shimmering sea. The scent of rotting sea algae filled the humid air mixed with wafts of greasy sunblock cream and the occasional spicy aroma of Thai street food that had been carried in small plastic packets onto the boat.

Harry, Euclid, and Sarah found a spot to sit down, away from the chatty tourists and locals napping on the shaded lower levels of the boat. As they settled into the plastic chairs screwed into the upper deck, the scene ahead was already turning into a picture-postcard view, with the looming silhouette of Koh Phangan framed by a sky ablaze with pink and orange.

"Thanks for convincing me to come, Sarah. The Full Moon Party is going to make for some great content on my travel blog," Harry said, snapping a few photos with her phone.

Euclid chuckled. "I'm still not entirely sold on the idea, you know. But I do have a few days to decide, right?"

Sarah nudged him playfully. "Exactly! In the meantime, let's just enjoy the beaches. And I know you're itching to go diving."

"Yeah," Euclid said, grinning. "I've heard that Sail Rock and Chumphon Pinnacle are must-visits. Those spots are rich in marine life, and if we're lucky, we might have a chance to see some whale sharks."

"You'll have to go alone on that trip, Euclid," Sarah said, looking serious. "You know I'm not the world's best swimmer, and I feel so nervous on small boats, especially if there are sharks around. I prefer to explore inland."

Harry's eyes lit up. "That sounds amazing! I've read about some stunning waterfalls on the island."

Sarah's eyes widened. "That's an excellent idea. How about we hike through the jungle to see them? Sounds to me like that would be a day well spent."

Sarah leaned back in her chair, her eyes following the raucous seagulls swooping and circling the boat. "So, Harry, what's the name of the resort we're staying at?"

"Mango Moon Hideaway," Harry replied, scrolling through her phone to pull up a picture. "It's a bit secluded, but a high school friend of mine is staying there right now, and she's recommended it."

"That's amazing! Why didn't you mention we were going to meet a friend of yours?"

Harry hesitated, lost for words. "To be honest, Zoë is not a real friend of mine. We grew up in the same town, Ithaca, went to high school together and even worked as reporters in New York, but somehow, we never clicked. She's just..." Harry's mouth grimaced in discomfort. "It's hard to say what's wrong with her, but you'll meet her, so I don't want to prejudice your opinion. You'll see for yourself. It's hard to explain why Zoë rubs me the wrong way. Anyway, she's also a travel blogger, and she told me the place is a hidden gem. Apparently, you can just lay in a hammock on your porch and let the sound of the waves lull you to sleep. I've seen photos on her Instagram."

Sarah's eyes closed briefly, picturing the scene. "Oh, that sounds absolutely divine."

Harry hadn't been perfectly honest with her friends when she said that Zoë had merely recommended Mango Moon Hideaway. Zoë had written to Harry a few days earlier and demanded her help. Her DMs were cryptic, but the plea for assistance was clear.

I know we have not always seen eye to eye, but I've just noticed that you're nearby, and I need help from someone I can trust. I can't explain what it is about, but it's big! This story will set us up for life. See the Google location of the resort where I'm staying below. I hope you can make it. Don't tell anyone that I'm a reporter! See you soon!

Harry was still feeling indignant about how Zoë had assumed that Harry would rush to her assistance, but then, in all fairness, she could not resist a good story. What was Zoë was investigating? She was too close to just pass up on this opportunity. While Harry enjoyed her travel blogging, she had to admit that it was not intellectually challenging. She often struggled to make a fun story out of a mundane sightseeing trip.

Euclid, who had been absorbed with his phone, interrupted Harry's ruminations. "Okay, so I've found the place online. It looks like it's perched right on the hills, overlooking the sea. The restaurant and swimming pool are on the cliff itself, and the huts are spread out below, each surrounded by mango and banana trees. It has some pretty solid reviews, mostly from backpackers. Listen to this one: *Epic Foam Parties!*"

Sarah raised an eyebrow, her eyes twinkling with curiosity. "Foam party? What on earth is a foam party?"

Euclid chuckled. "Ah, the classic foam party. The pinnacle of human civilization," he said. "Imagine a swimming pool, but it's filled with foam instead of water. People enter said foam-filled pool and dance around like they're auditioning for a laundry detergent commercial. It's truly an unforgettable experience."

Harry burst into laughter. "A laundry detergent commercial? Oh, you're such a poet, Euclid."

"Hey, it's not my cup of tea, but to each their own," he continued, grinning. "Personally, I prefer my pool water without bubbles and my parties without the risk of accidentally getting soap in my eyes."

"Well, I'm with you on that one," Harry said, joining in. "Foam parties might not be so 'epic', but the resort itself sounds amazing."

"As long as there's an option to not be covered in foam, I think we'll manage," Sarah said, her eyes meeting Harry's.

As the ferry approached Koh Phangan, the three young friends couldn't help but marvel at the island's natural beauty. Verdant hills met the horizon, fringed by shimmering golden beaches that seemed to stretch on forever. Palm trees stood like sentinels along the coastline; beyond them, the dense jungle beckoned with the promise of undiscovered adventures.

Amid the clatter of footsteps and the rustle of bags being gathered by the other passengers, Sarah turned to Harry. "Have you had any luck tracking down the captain of the boat where your parents... you know?"

Harry shook her head, her eyes never leaving the increasingly clear view of the approaching island. "I've got a name, but it's a common one. I hope to ask around when we get there—maybe in some bars or restaurants where the locals hang out."

"Why don't you use Google Translate to search for Thai newspaper articles about the accident?" Euclid chimed in. "It could help, right?"

Harry sighed. "I've tried that. But you know how it is with translations. They don't always make sense. Sometimes, it turns into an incomprehensible mess, and I don't want to make any assumptions based on a bad translation."

Sarah placed her hand reassuringly on Harry's arm. "Well, I hope you find the truth. I can only imagine how much it means to you."

Harry nodded, her eyes now filled with a mix of hope and resolve. "Yeah, me too. Either way, I won't stop looking."

As the ferry docked, the chatter of excited tourists and local commuters filled the air. The three friends grabbed their bags and joined the throng of passengers as they disembarked. Their thoughts were already focused on the adventures awaiting them on Koh Phangan.

The island port buzzed with activity as they left the ferry behind. A kaleidoscope of sights and sounds greeted them as they made their way along the lively quayside. Friendly locals hawked fresh fruits, trinkets, and island maps from makeshift stalls. Travelers—backpackers with dreadlocks, young families with excited kids, and couples holding hands—milled around, their faces flushed with the prospect of the island's many adventures. An army of tuk-tuks, taxis, and scooter rental stands lined the perimeter of the harbor, each manned by keen tour operators who vied for the tourists' attention by means of enthusiastic gestures and calls.

"Wow, this is quite the bustling little harbor," Harry observed, soaking in the atmosphere.

"Yeah, it's got everything from coconuts to sarongs," Euclid agreed. "Speaking of which, we should head to one of those scooter rental places if we want to explore the whole island."

Sarah pointed to a row of shops just beyond the queue of taxis. "Those look promising."

The trio navigated their way through the throngs of people and headed towards the scooter stands. Each rental spot was adorned with various models, all displayed like proud trophies by the stall owners. Rental rates were posted on colorful boards, typically accompanied by pictures of idyllic island destinations to entice potential customers.

"Should we go basic or sporty?" Sarah wondered out loud, eyeing the options.

"Basic is fine by me. We're not entering a Grand Prix," Harry joked.

Euclid laughed. "Agreed. As long as they get us from point A to point B."

After a brief negotiation over the daily rental price and a quick tutorial on how to operate them, they each picked a scooter, strapped on their open-face, retro-style helmets, and set off. As they left the port behind, Harry couldn't help but feel that this was the beginning of something unforgettable. With the wind in their hair and the smell of the ocean filling their senses, they rode steadily towards Mango Moon Hideaway, Euclid leading the way, his phone securely mounted on his handlebar for easy navigation.

They soon turned off the main road, leaving the bustling port area behind, and entered a quiet track shrouded by lush jungle. A dappled canopy of leaves overhead filtered the bright sunlight, casting playful shadows across the dirt trail. Their scooters hummed along in harmony with the songs of cicadas and exotic birds, which seemed to playfully guide them deeper into the island's tropical heart.

"Wow, this is stunning!" Sarah called out from behind Harry, her eyes wide with wonder. "Look at all the colors!"

Indeed, the track was flanked by an explosion of tropical flora—wild orchids with their vibrant hues, ruby-red hibiscus flowers, and flamboyant plumeria in whites and pinks. They rode past groves of coconut palms and towering rubber trees, their leaves shimmering in the occasional shafts of piercing sunlight that broke through the canopy.

As they climbed a steep hill, the forest began to thin, offering flashing glimpses of the cerulean sea below. Harry's heart swelled as they reached the top, where a viewpoint clearing revealed a breathtaking panorama: a sparkling blue-green bay on one side and, in the distance, the misty majestic silhouettes of Koh Tao and Koh Nang Yuan. The sight was so beautiful and tranquil that Harry momentarily forgot the dark question that had originally brought her to Thailand.

After soaking in the view and taking some photos, they descended the other side of the hill, following the winding trail indicated on Euclid's phone. Before long, a rustic wooden sign came into view, with the words 'Mango Moon Hideaway' hand-painted in bright colors.

As they rode through the entrance to the resort compound, it was clear they had arrived at a slice of paradise. Nestled among the jungle foliage, the resort was a secluded haven. The restaurant and pool area were perched atop a small cliff with a panoramic view of the sea and surrounding islands. Wooden huts, each adorned with a small porch and a hammock, were tucked away below the cliff, almost hidden by a curtain of tropical greenery.

"Wow," Sarah said, breathing heavily as they dismounted their scooters. "This place is divine."

Harry grinned, taking off her helmet. "I told you it was worth the ride."

Walking toward the reception area, they passed clusters of young people, their skin slightly pink from sun and saltwater. Towels were draped over their youthful shoulders or tied around slender waists. A couple of young lovers supported each other by the elbow as they shook the sand out of their flip-flops, while others chatted and laughed under the trees, recounting tales of their underwater adventures.

"Hey, how's it going?" one guy greeted them, waving cheerfully, a surfboard tucked under his arm. "Welcome to paradise!"

"Thank you!" Harry replied, returning the wave. "We've just arrived. I'm Harry, and these are my friends, Euclid and Sarah."

"Nice to meet you all. I'm Grove." The young man put the surfboard down and insouciantly pulled his blonde hair into a perky ponytail.

"Where do we check in?"

"The reception is on the main deck, just over there," he said, pointing to a large wooden structure perched on the cliff. "See you around, guys."

As they reached the deck, they saw the sea sprawling endlessly before them. Sarah let out a low whistle. "This is incredible. Can you imagine waking up to this every day?"

"It really is paradise," Harry agreed, feeling the sea breeze on her face and letting her eyes linger on the horizon where sky kissed water.

The reception office was tucked away at the back of the deck, a cozy little nook filled with useful travel brochures and maps. A friendly-looking receptionist was sitting behind a bamboo counter, but what caught Harry's eye was the glass-fronted fridge standing to the side of it. It was filled with an assortment of cold beverages—from coconut water to local beers.

"Hey, check this out," she said to Sarah, who was still captivated by the view. Harry gestured toward a handwritten note taped to the fridge. "They've got an honor system here. You just jot down what you took and your name and they add it to your bill later."

Sarah walked over and read the note. "That's so trusting. I love how laid-back this place seems."

Both of them felt a wave of relaxation wash over them.

"*Sawasdee kha.* Welcome to Mango Moon Hideaway!" the petite Thai woman with a heart-shaped face said, greeting them warmly as they approached the reception counter. "My name's Somchai, and you must be Harry, Sarah, and Euclid. We've been expecting you."

"Thank you, Somchai," Harry replied, taking in her kind eyes and inviting smile. "We're thrilled to be here."

Somchai handed them their keys. "Your reserved accommodation is down this way, on the cliffside, not far from the beach. Would you please follow me?"

As they prepared to leave the reception area, Harry noticed a colorful flyer for a Thai cooking class tucked in among other tourist information pamphlets. She picked up the paper and showed it to Sarah. "What do you think? A cooking class might be a fun way to immerse ourselves in Thai culture."

"Sounds amazing," Sarah agreed. "The food in Thailand has been so good; it would be great to learn how to make some of it ourselves."

They followed Somchai down a stepped gravel pathway framed by lush tropical vegetation descending towards the beach. The air grew thicker with the briny scent of the ocean as they reached their small one-room huts.

"As you can see, each hut comes with its own bathroom and a hammock to enjoy the view," Somchai explained, setting down their bags. "If you need anything else, please don't hesitate to ask."

"It's all wonderful," Sarah said. "By the way, your English is impeccable. Did you learn it here on the island?" the English teacher in Sarah couldn't help but ask.

Somchai blushed a little. "Thank you so much. I went to an American school in Bangkok. I grew up there, but I prefer the slow pace of the islands."

"I don't blame you," Sarah answered.

Just as Somchai was turning to leave, a booming voice echoed from the top of the path. "Ah, fresh faces! Welcome, welcome to paradise!"

Harry, Sarah, and Euclid turned around in unison to see a tall, slightly overweight man with dark, thick hair sauntering towards them. He carried himself with an air of self-assurance that bordered on arrogance.

"Reggie's the name, and this is my sanctuary, my Utopia, my Eden, if you will!" He stretched out his arms as if he were embracing the horizon. "Bet you've never seen anything quite like it."

Harry couldn't shake off the feeling that she had seen Reggie before; his tall stature, muscular build, and dandy appearance reminded her of someone, but she couldn't put her finger on who.

"It's beautiful," Sarah said politely.

"Beautiful? My dear, it's magnificent, awe-inspiring, a marvel of modern hospitality. Took all my money to carve this Eden out of the wilderness."

Harry and Euclid exchanged glances, clearly picking up on Reggie's pompous demeanor. It was when she heard his Australian accent that she realized who Reggie reminded her of.

"It's wonderful," Harry finally said. "I'm sure it has taken many years to develop this resort."

"Years? No, I don't have that much patience. I opened the place two years ago, and it was an immediate success. We've been featured in top travel magazines around the world as a must-stay-and-see destination in the Gulf of Thailand." He winked exaggeratedly and turned back up the path. "Enjoy your stay!"

As Reggie's voice trailed off, Somchai rolled her eyes and then smiled at the guests. "If there's anything you need, please let us know. Have a wonderful time."

Somchai was about to head back to the reception when she remembered something.

"By the way, we are having a crab feast tonight on the restaurant deck if you'd like to come. One of our guests has generously purchased three cases of fresh crab and has asked our chef to prepare something special for everyone to share," Somchai informed them before ascending to the reception area.

"That sounds wonderful," Sarah said. "Are you coming, Harry?"

"Yes, of course. It sounds like it might be fun. By the way, don't you think that Reggie looks just like Matt Preston? He could be his twin brother."

"Harry, you know very well I don't follow celebrities." Euclid gave his friend a look of fake indignation.

"He has no idea who Matt Preston is," Sarah added, laughing at her boyfriend's ignorance concerning minor celebrities. "But I agree with you. Reggie does look like that tall guy who used to be the judge on MasterChef Australia. The resemblance is uncanny."

Harry, Euclid, and Sarah retreated into their respective huts to rest and freshen up, each pondering Reggie's larger-than-life personality.

CHAPTER 2

A CRAB FEAST

As the golden hues of the sunset painted the sky crimson, the evening came alive with the melodic chirping of local birds and insects. Harry could hear the calls of the Oriental Magpie-Robin, a sweet, tuneful sound that blended with the whispering wind and lapping waves. She felt a deep sense of contentment as she lay in her hammock, swaying gently back and forth with a book in hand. The beauty of the nature around her made it hard for Harry to concentrate on the pages of her detective novel.

Just as the sun dipped below the horizon, casting the last of its tropical warmth over the ocean, a figure appeared on the path leading past her hut. A young man, seemingly in his mid-twenties, trudged by, looking a bit worn out from the day's tropical heat. His T-shirt was faded, almost distressed, though Harry quickly wondered if it was by artful design rather than from just frequent wear. A large backpack weighed down his shoulders.

He caught her gaze and offered a warm, if somewhat weary, smile. "Hello there! You must be me new neighbor!" he called out, his voice marked by a strong Irish accent.

"Hi," Harry replied, setting her book aside and sitting up. "Have you just arrived?"

"Well, I've made the Hideaway my temporary home, but I had to nip over to the mainland for a few days. Just got off the ferry from Surat Thani an hour ago," he said, dropping his backpack to the ground with a sigh of relief. "What a journey that was—five hours on a boat packed to the rafters with locals heading home and tourists like meself. It was a real mix of cultures, so it was. The sea was a bit choppy, felt like a never-ending rollercoaster. But the views were stunning, especially as we passed the smaller islands."

"Wow, that sounds both exhausting and amazing," Harry said, sympathizing with his fatigue.

"A bit of both, to be honest. I'm Connor, by the way," he said, extending his hand.

"Harry," she replied, shaking it. "Nice to meet you, Connor. How long are you staying here?"

"As long as the island will have me—or until me wallet gives out, whichever comes first," he joked, picking up his backpack again. "This place is something special, that's why I've come back."

"It's my first time here, but I'm inclined to agree with you," Harry said. "It's like another world."

"That it is, Harry. That it is," Connor agreed, his eyes lingering on the now-darkening horizon. "Well, I better get settled in. Maybe I'll catch you around?"

"Actually, Connor, you should come up to the restaurant deck later. They're hosting a free crab feast tonight," Harry suggested, seeing the opportunity to socialize and perhaps make a new friend on the island.

"Ah, the lady in reception mentioned that," Connor said, scratching his head as he considered the idea. "Wasn't quite sure if it is bang on my scene, but if you'll be there, I reckon it might be a good craic. But I won't be trying any crab... the old allergy is brutal."

"Absolutely, everything's better when you're not doing it alone. I'm sure there will be other food to try," Harry said encouragingly.

"Alright, you've convinced me. I just need to take a shower and scrub off the journey. I'll join everyone up there after eight. Sound good?"

"Sounds like a plan. See you there," Harry replied, flashing a friendly smile.

"See you there, Harry," Connor echoed, picking up his backpack and making his way toward his own hut.

For a moment, Harry considered returning to her book but decided instead to explore her surroundings briefly before dinner. She left her hut and meandered along the winding path leading up to the deck, charmed by the glow of whimsical solar lanterns dotting the garden. They swayed gently in the evening breeze, casting dancing shadows on the tropical foliage below.

She reached the deck and paused, captivated by the ethereal beauty before her. The atmosphere was almost magical. Waves crashed softly against the shore behind her, creating a rhythmic backdrop to the murmur of conversation and the lilting tunes of soft music that wafted across the deck. Her senses were immediately enveloped by the intoxicating aroma of Thai cuisine—hints of garlic and ginger mingled with the tangy scent of lime and lemongrass. The air was also infused with the smoky richness of grilled seafood.

Through the open kitchen window, she saw the Thai chef immersed in a whirlwind of culinary activity. The clanging of pots and pans mingled with the sizzle of ingredients hitting hot oil. *I'm so happy I came here*, Harry thought, feeling a sense of peace and contentment but also a dash of apprehension about meeting Zoë. *What is the big story that Zoë's investigating?*

Spotting Sarah sitting across the deck, Harry returned her enthusiastic wave and began making her way over, eager to join her friends for the feast. But just as she was about to step forward, her gaze shifted and fell upon a figure in a corner of the deck. The short black hair and the tight black dress stood out in a crowd dressed in flowery summer dresses and loose yoga pants. Her old colleague Zoë had always had a slightly gothic sense of fashion. Harry had found it a little over-the-top, if not dramatic, but it was Zoë's hallmark.

I must talk to her.

As she walked closer, Harry decided to keep up a pretense that their meeting was incidental. If Zoë was hiding her true identity from others, she would not want to reveal too much in public.

"Zoë! Fancy meeting you here!" Harry exclaimed. "What a coincidence!"

Zoë looked up sharply at the sound of Harry's voice.

"Oh my God! Is that you, Harry? What's with the pink hair?"

"Yes, it's me. And what's with the comment? I like my pink hair, you know. Some people say it suits me."

"Ever so sensitive," Zoë remarked, which made Harry remember why they never got along when they worked together at the magazine.

But there was no time to retort as Zoë pulled Harry aside, away from the tables, her eyes darting around to ensure no one was eavesdropping. "Listen, Harry, you must not tell anyone my real job. It's imperative," she whispered urgently.

Harry's mind was racing with questions. "I guessed that much from your message. What's going on, Zoë? What are you doing here?"

Zoë's eyes scanned the area one more time before locking onto Harry's. "I can't explain everything now, but I've been investigating a story, and it's brought me here."

"What's the story?"

"I'll tell you soon, but for now, think big, Anna Delvey big. I could become really famous once I publish it. There is enough material for a book or even a movie, or a Netflix documentary. But for now, you must keep this a secret. Promise me, Harry."

Harry looked at her old colleague, sensing the seriousness of the situation in her eyes, and nodded. "Alright, Zoë. I promise. But why did you ask me to come here? What do you need me for?"

Zoë took a long drag on her strawberry-flavored vape, exhaling slowly before she spoke. "Look, Harry, I've spent over a year collecting evidence and following up on clues. The Mango Moon Hideaway is not what it seems, and I hope to catch some people red-handed during the Full Moon Party. I'm going to set up a trap, and I will need your help to document the event."

Harry's eyes narrowed slightly. "A trap for what?"

Zoë smirked, a touch of arrogance creeping into her expression. "I can't reveal all the details, obviously. Just know that it will be big, not just some vacuous blog about travel tips or food reviews," she said, insinuating that her journalism was somehow superior to Harry's travel blogging.

She'd always known Zoë to be cutthroat and competitive when they had worked together at the New York magazine. Zoë had a knack for making the workplace uncomfortable, but there was no denying her journalistic skills.

"I see," Harry replied cautiously, letting the subtle insult slide. "Well, your secret is safe with me, but I will need to have more details before I agree to anything. Just curious: Are we in any danger?"

Zoë took another drag from her vape, her eyes veiled. "I don't think so. I've covered my tracks very well. No one suspects anything. You can go on enjoying your crab feast and moonlit beaches with your little friends, and we'll chat as soon as I've devised the *denouement* of my story. I want it to be epic. Just remember, you promised not to blow my cover."

"Of course," Harry nodded. "You always did love diving in at the deep end."

Zoë put her vape away into a fashionable clutch bag and glanced at Harry with a condescending smile. "And you always did know how to float through life effortlessly. Enjoy your evening. We'll talk later."

As Zoë retreated back to the edge of the deck, Harry felt a slightly frustrated mix of intrigue and caution settle over her.

She approached Sarah, Euclid, and Connor, who were leaning against a wooden balustrade, deep in conversation. "Hey, guys. Looks like you've all met my new neighbor." She nodded towards Connor, who raised his glass in a half-toast, half-salute.

Sarah's eyes followed Harry's gaze. "Ah, the infamous neighbor. You collect them wherever you go, don't you?" She laughed before her expression turned curious. "Was that woman you were talking to earlier the friend you had told us about? Why doesn't she join us?"

Caught off guard, Harry hesitated for a moment. She didn't want to lie to Sarah but also didn't want to expose Zoë's undercover operation. "Um, yes, it's her, but...let's say she's an acquired taste."

Sensing Harry's reticence, Sarah didn't push the point. "Alright, if she's not great company, no worries. We have plenty of good company here already," she said, gesturing at the small gathering.

Euclid, who had been deeply engrossed in a conversation with Connor about scuba diving sites, interjected, "Well, should we take our seats? They've set up a communal table for tonight's crab feast."

The group agreed and moved towards the tables arranged into a large U-shape. The nearly full moon, a glowing waxing gibbous orb, cast its metallic light over the deck as if ushering them into the evening's festivities. Aromas of grilled seafood mixed with undertones of lemongrass and coconut filled the air.

Harry couldn't help but feel grateful for the night that lay ahead, full of delicious food and congenial company. But Zoë's secrecy scratched at the back of her mind.

Harry, Connor, Sarah, and Euclid took seats opposite a middle-aged couple, their faces warm and inviting.

The woman smiled at the group and introduced herself as Dominique. Her sun-kissed blonde hair and a scattering of freckles across her nose exuded a sense of athletic energy.

"Thank you for joining us," she said. "This is my husband, Pierre."

Pierre was slightly older and also blond but had a bold patch of pink skin visible through his thinning hair.

"Ah, *bonsoir*! *Bonsoir*!" Pierre exclaimed, leaning over the table to shake hands with each of Harry's friends. "We are—ah, how you say—very 'appy, yes, that you have joined us for this *fête* of crabs!"

Dominique cut in, her eyes twinkling. "Ah, *oui*, let me explain. We were, um, promenading in the port, when a *pêcheur*, um, fisherman, yes, he approaches us. He had these *magnifiques* crabs! He was supposed to sell them to a restaurant, but, ah, the owner changed his mind!"

"Yes, yes," Pierre chimed in, nodding enthusiastically. "So, what could we do? We decided to make a *bon marché*—a good deal! We bought *tres caisses* to help this poor man out. *Et voilà!* Now, we have a feast!"

The couple's enthusiasm was infectious, and Harry couldn't help but smile. The mix of French and English, their warm accents, and the slightly off-kilter grammar all added to the charm of the evening.

Euclid leaned forward and grinned. "That's incredibly kind of you both. I'm Euclid, and this is Sarah. We're both teachers from Seoul."

Pierre looked at Sarah for a moment, a little befuddled. "Ah, you are Thai, *non*?"

Sarah laughed heartily at the innocent mistake. "No, no, I'm actually Korean American, but you're not the first to think that. When we landed in Bangkok, I went to a street market, and a vendor tried to give me a local discount on some silk scarves. She started speaking to me in Thai; she was so confident I belonged there!"

"And?" Dominique prompted, clearly entertained.

Sarah's eyes sparkled with amusement. "Well, not wanting to disappoint her, I just nodded and smiled, thinking she'd get the hint. But no, she then proceeded to ask me some detailed questions. I had to finally confess, and let's just say, the 'local discount' evaporated pretty quickly!"

The table erupted into laughter, the atmosphere growing ever more convivial. Pierre clapped his hands together and exclaimed, "Ah, *la confusion ethnique*, it only happens to the best of us, *n'est-ce pas?*"

Balancing a massive platter of cooked Thai chili crab with grace and ease, Somchai interrupted the laughter and chatter. "Everyone, please may I have your attention for a moment? I don't want to keep you waiting for this delicious feast, but I must say a big 'thank you' to Pierre and Dominique for their generosity tonight."

Harry scanned the table; the excitement was palpable among the roughly twenty individuals present, each lit by the soft illumination of the many lanterns hanging from the rafters above. Zoë, however, was almost shrouded in darkness at the far end of the table. She seemed deeply engrossed in a conversation with someone. Harry looked closely and recognized the long, blonde hair—it was the surfer dude she had met upon arrival at the Hideaway. Harry's curiosity briefly flared but was soon extinguished as Pierre stood up, glass in hand.

"Ah, *mes amis*, it's our pleasure, really. You see, Dominique and I are here on our second honeymoon. We've been married for twenty-five years." He paused to give his wife a loving glance. "And what better place to renew our vows matrimonial than this beautiful island?"

"Thank you, everyone, for joining us," Dominique chimed in, capturing everyone's attention effortlessly as she searched for her words. "We wanted to celebrate our anniversary but did not want to make a lot of... err... fuss. So, this is perfect! *Une célébration très impromptue.* A gathering of strangers sharing time and a meal in this special location. When I was thinking of what to say tonight, I found this quote online: 'Strangers are a family you are yet to know.' I hope you enjoy this meal and time together."

A symphony of clinking glasses filled the air as everyone lifted their drinks for a toast. "To love, to life, and to unexpected feasts!" Pierre exclaimed.

Everyone now raised their glasses. Calls of *Cheers* and *Santé* echoed from the guests.

Somchai carefully set the first crab platter down in front of Dominique and Pierre. "Our chef has prepared the fresh crab in three traditional Thai ways for you to enjoy," she announced, her eyes gleaming with pride.

"First, we have *Poo Phad Phong Karee*, which is crab stir-fried with yellow curry. It's creamy, with a hint of spice and sweetness. Next, we have *Tom Yum Poo*, a crab version of our famous Thai sour and spicy soup. Finally, for those who prefer something a bit simpler, we have *Poo Neung Manao*: crab steamed with a spicy lime garlic sauce."

Several of the kitchen staff followed Somchai, setting down more platters on the long tables. Alongside the crab entrées, there were side dishes aplenty: jasmine rice, Thai cucumber salad, spicy green papaya salad, stir-fried morning glory, and an array of traditional sauces.

The party atmosphere was enlivened by the sounds of wine bottles being opened and the clinking of beer bottles. Amidst the merry chatter, the distant sound of waves crashing on the shoreline provided a comforting backdrop.

Sitting next to Harry, Euclid eagerly grabbed a whole crab from one of the platters, then hesitated, looking slightly bewildered on how he should proceed. Pierre, noticing his predicament, chuckled warmly.

"Ah, *mon ami*, let me show you how to enjoy this delicacy." With experienced hands, Pierre picked up a crab. "You see, first you break off the legs and claws, like so. Then, you can use a small fork or your fingers to extract the meat. For the body, you open it in half, and voila! Don't forget, the 'crab butter' in the shell is a delicacy."

Euclid followed Pierre's lead, visibly relieved and excited to dig in. Around them, the table burst into conversation and laughter, the delicious food fueling a sense of community and joy that transcended language barriers and geographical origins. It was a magical evening on Koh Phangan that none of them would likely forget any time soon.

Sarah took a bite of the *Poo Phad Phong Karee*, and her eyes lit up. "Oh my God, this is heavenly. The flavors are just amazing!"

Harry nodded in agreement, her own mouth full of the tangy and spicy *Tom Yum*. "Absolutely. We should definitely do some cooking classes. Can you imagine being able to make this at home? Plus, it would make a killer blog post." She was already envisioning the vivid, colorful photos she would take of the ingredients and finished dishes—sure to attract a surge in readers and engagement.

Sitting opposite them, Dominique overheard their conversation, her eyes twinkling. "Did I hear you two talking about cooking classes? May I join you? Thai cuisine is so fascinating! All these herbs and spices—I have not heard of many of them. It's so different from what we use in France."

Harry and Sarah exchanged a quick look, and then both nodded enthusiastically. "Of course, Dominique! We would love you to join us," Sarah said.

Harry turned to Euclid, who had been absorbed in deconstructing a piece of steamed crab. "How about you, Euclid? Are you interested in becoming one of the cooking brigade?"

He shook his head, grinning. "You know, as tempting as that sounds, I saw a poster at the reception about swimming with whale sharks. I've always wanted to do that. If you're doing the cooking class, I think that's my opportunity to do that instead."

Connor, who was enjoying a shellfish-free tofu dish especially prepared for him, suddenly looked up, his interest piqued. "Did you say whale sharks? That sounds like an adventure. Mind if I tag along?"

"Definitely. The more the merrier," Euclid replied, echoing Sarah's enthusiasm. "How about you, Pierre? Do you feel like joining us in the deep blue to meet some whale sharks?"

Pierre laughed, shaking his head as he sipped his wine. "Ah, *non, non*. Sharks are not for me. I prefer my adventures on land. Perhaps a long hike across this beautiful island, *oui*? The nature here is as captivating as the sea."

Everyone nodded in agreement. As the evening progressed, the guests continued to bond over their shared experience of the island and the adventures that lay ahead.

CHAPTER 3

HIDDEN AWAY

The beam of a powerful electric torch cut a narrow path through the dense foliage and the darkness of the Koh Phangan jungle, casting eerie shadows across the surrounding vegetation. The muffled sounds of laughter and chatter from the party back at the Hideaway deck drifted through the air, a world away from the solitude of this secluded trail.

"This is the perfect time," the figure whispered, holding the torch with a grip that was a little too tight, a little too tense. "Everyone's distracted, feasting and drinking. They won't notice I'm missing."

The person making their way cautiously through the darkness counted out each step, "Eighteen, nineteen, twenty." Reaching the twentieth step, they took a sharp right turn at a massive boulder that served as an unspoken landmark along the trail. "Almost there," they reassured themselves apprehensively. "Just a few more steps."

The torchlight cast unsettling patterns on the ground as it revealed a narrower path ahead. Another fifty steps, another turn, and then the cave appeared in the torch's glow. The sight should have been comforting—it was the intended destination, after all—but instead, it sent a shiver down the figure's spine.

Vigilantly, the individual paused to look around, eyes darting and ears straining for any sign of movement or noise. Every snapped twig or small animal rustling in the foliage sounded like a gunshot in the still air. *Is someone following me? No, it's just my mind playing tricks*, they thought, gulping down a wave of fear.

"Let's hope you're still safe and sound," the silhouette muttered to no one in particular. With a trembling hand, they pushed aside a flat stone blocking the entrance, large enough to be a deterrent but not so large as to arouse suspicion.

As the stone ground against the earth, opening a dark void into the cave, an overwhelming sense of urgency flooded over the figure. *Not much longer*, they thought, stepping into the pitch-black cavern, the torchlight flickering ominously as if warning of an inescapable doom.

And then they were swallowed by the darkness, leaving the world outside to its blissful ignorance. The sound of the distant party was now a haunting lullaby for whatever lay within the cave.

CHAPTER 4

COOK LIKE A THAI

The next day, as Sarah, Harry, Dominique, and a few others gathered around the entrance of a traditional Thai cottage, the atmosphere was one of eager anticipation. The cottage's wooden walls were adorned with traditional Thai ornaments, and the glossy colors of hanging herbs and spices in wicker baskets and the intoxicating aroma of fresh vegetables set a jovial mood for what promised to be an unforgettable culinary experience.

Just then, a petite Thai woman with a beaming smile stepped out from the cottage onto the porch. Her ease and confidence suggested years of culinary mastery. She wore a colorful sarong and a loose-fitting blouse, and her raven hair was tied back neatly.

"*Sawasdee kha*!" she greeted gently, bringing her hands together in a traditional Thai *wai*. "Welcome to my humble kitchen! My name is Areeya, and I'll be your guide through the fascinating world of Thai cuisine today. I'm thrilled you've decided to join me."

Areeya's English was excellent, tinged only slightly by a melodic Thai accent. Her eyes sparkled with genuine enthusiasm as she continued to speak to the group of culinary apprentices.

"Today, we're going to explore some of the foundational elements of Thai cooking. We'll delve into the art of balancing flavors—salty, sweet, sour, and spicy. You'll also get some hands-on experience in making some of Thailand's most beloved dishes."

She clapped her hands together excitedly. "Are you all ready to spice up your life a little? Please, follow me."

Areeya led the group inside the cottage, which opened up into a spacious and well-organized kitchen. A series of wooden countertops were set along the walls, decked with cutting boards, a colorful array of fresh vegetables, and all sorts of mysterious jars filled with spices and sauces. The room was alive with the aromatic promise of a superb culinary adventure.

As the group took their places around a large central table, Areeya distributed aprons, and the air filled with the chatter of excited voices. Sarah, Harry, and Dominique shared friendly glances, smiles on their faces.

Areeya directed the group's attention to a beautiful display of herbs, each one presented in its own small dish, accompanied by a label written both in English and Thai. "These are the soul of our cuisine," she said, with a twinkle in her eye. "They bring layers of flavor and aroma to our uniquely Thai dishes. Let's start with this one. This is Thai basil."

Harry found it difficult to concentrate on the demonstration as her mind was preoccupied with the revelations from the previous night's conversation with Zoë. One name in particular had kept Harry tossing and turning all night. Zoë suggested there was an impostor or a con artist at the Hideaway, someone on the scale of Anna Delvey. She didn't need to spell it out for Harry. The name Anna Delvey, or Anna Sorokin as she was officially known, was familiar to any journalist or reporter in New York City.

Sorokin was a working-class Russian who had embedded herself in New York high society by pretending to be an heiress to a large European fortune. She exploited gullible socialites and swindled hundreds of thousands of dollars from them while living in five-star hotels and enjoying an extravagant lifestyle. Sorokin was eventually arrested, thanks to the evidence gathered by a supposed friend—a reporter named Williams—whom she had also cheated out of a large sum of money.

Was Zoë imagining herself to be another Williams? Probably. But who was the impostor? So far, everyone she had met at the Hideaway seemed kind and generous. It was hard to imagine that there was a fraudster amidst them.

"As you can see, each of these herbs has its own unique flavor profile," Areeya summarized her descriptions, and Harry felt guilty for not listening more attentively.

"When combined, they create the complex and balanced flavors that Thai cuisine is renowned for. Alright, now that we've gotten to know our herbs a bit, let's put them to good use, shall we?"

Everyone nodded in agreement, their senses awakened and palates tingling, ready to dive into the next phase of their Thai culinary masterclass.

"Today, we'll be learning how to make a traditional Thai Green Curry or *Kaeng Khiao Wan*," Areeya announced, beaming as she unveiled a basket of ingredients.

"So, let's start with our curry paste. You can buy pre-made green curry paste at the store, but making it fresh makes all the difference," Areeya announced. "Any questions before we begin?"

Dominique asked, "Is it okay to use regular basil if we can't find Thai basil?"

Areeya smiled. "It won't be exactly the same, but it'll do in an emergency. The important thing is to enjoy the cooking process and the meal you've created."

Areeya circulated among the participants, her eyes scanning for any signs of confusion or hesitation. "How are we doing here?" she asked Harry and Sarah, who were busy chopping herbs.

"We're good," Harry replied. "I'm just trying to cut the lemongrass as thin as possible."

"Nice! The finer you chop it, the easier it'll blend into a smooth paste."

She moved on to Dominique and her partner, who appeared to be struggling a bit with peeling the galangal. "Ah, let me show you a little trick," Areeya said, taking a piece.

"*Merci*, that helps a lot," Dominique exclaimed, visibly relieved.

As the pairs continued to measure and chop their ingredients, a symphony of scents filled the air. The sharp aroma of chilies mixed with the earthy smell of spices and the fragrant bouquets of fresh herbs.

Amid the sound of cutting and chopping, the women engaged in gentle gossip.

"So, what brings you to Koh Phangan?" Dominique inquired.

"Well, Euclid and I are here on vacation. We want to explore as much of Asia as we can while we're working in Seoul. Once we go back to the States, I think it will be too expensive for us to come here. We're only teachers," Sarah explained. "We met Harry on Koh Samui at a yoga retreat. There was a... terrible accident. Anyway, as we were leaving Koh Samui, it turned out that Harry had some business to attend to here, so we came together."

"*Un* business?" Dominique asked.

"Not a real business," Harry clarified. "I'm trying to find out what happened to my parents. They were working for Doctors Without Borders, and they died in a boating accident twenty years ago not far from here."

"*Je suis vraiment désolée*," Dominique expressed her condolences. "Are they buried here?"

"No, their ashes were brought back to my grandparents' house where I grew up, but I need closure. I want to know exactly what happened, and so far, I'm finding conflicting accounts. There's no newspaper record of an American couple dying in a boating accident, and a teacher on Koh Samui told me that Doctors Without Borders doesn't work in this area. It's all a bit bizarre."

"I'm sure there's *une explication* for all this. I hope you find a solution. It must be *mélancolie* not knowing what happened to your loved ones."

"Thank you," Harry responded softly. "The captain of the boat that my parents were on when they died lives on Koh Phangan. I hope to find him and get all the details straight. It will put my mind at ease."

"I'm sure you'll find him. It's a small island. And how do you find the Hideaway so far?" Dominique changed the topic.

"I think it's quite amazing that Reggie built it all from scratch in just a few years. It's quite an investment," Harry said. "He must be quite the entrepreneur."

"You know, it's the American way," Dominique replied.

"What do you mean?"

"*Just do it!* and so on. The cowboy way," Dominique remarked, assuming her perspective was understood.

Harry didn't correct her that it was a Nike slogan and not one of the Founding Father's principles. The Europeans she had met tended to use stereotypes when referring to her countrymen.

"No, I mean, what do you mean by 'the American way'? I thought Reggie was Australian?" Harry was confused. Sarah listened eagerly, surprised by the revelation.

Dominique looked up from her cutting board.

"Oh, *non*, he's definitely American, but I've forgotten which part he's from. But it's true he's spent some time in Australia and picked up the accent. He worked there as a lookalike."

"A lookalike?" Sarah asked.

"It's when you resemble a celebrity, *un sosie*. You perform at parties and attend events. Believe it or not, it's a very well-paid job. If the celebrity is famous, you earn thousands of dollars per appearance. *Apparemment*, he resembles some Australian celebrity."

"Matt Preston!" Harry exclaimed. "It's true. His likeness is extraordinary."

"He lived there for a few years, but what's really funny is that he was on some sort of reality TV show," Dominique continued.

"Ah, that explains the showmanship!" Sarah chimed in. "From celebrity impersonator to reality TV and now a resort owner on an exotic island? Seriously?"

Dominique nodded and laughed. "Oh, *absolument*. He wrote about his journey in a self-help book. It's on Amazon. It has about four reviews next to a photo of Reggie in a silk ascot. He keeps copies in the office to hand out as party gifts to guests he wants to impress. He gave one to Pierre; it's called *Finding Your True Self*. It is a book *tres drôle* if you know the author and his 'true self'."

Harry rolled her eyes dramatically. "True Self? Sounds like someone loves massaging his own ego."

"*D'ailleurs*, I thought it was strange that he didn't stop by to say 'hello'," Dominique commented, referring to the previous night's party. "I felt it was a bit *discourtois*."

"Perhaps he was busy working on another book," Harry said, the suggestion making the women laugh, but she regretted the mean comment. Her grandmother used to tell her to be kind. *Everyone is fighting their own battle*, she would tell Harry whenever she made a cynical or sarcastic remark about others.

"Or maybe he does not enjoy not being the center of attention," Dominique speculated.

"That's quite possible. By the way, did you know Connor works for a big bank in Ireland? He's not even that old!" Sarah said, changing the subject.

Harry looked surprised. "Really? He doesn't strike me as the banking type. I assumed he was a student on a gap year."

Sarah grinned. "Oh, no. He isn't. He's a professional hacker. He develops security systems for banks and works remotely. Isn't that wild?"

Harry's eyes widened. "Wow, a hacker who develops bank security? That's interesting."

"And I spoke to your friend, Zoë, last night," Sarah continued excitedly. "She sent me the link to her blog. It's quite amazing. Have you read it?"

Harry felt a slight tinge of jealousy about Sarah praising her competition's blog. It was clear to Harry that Zoë had started the blog as a cover for her investigation. The idea that her archnemesis would run a successful travel blog simply to cover her tracks as she investigated a fraud made Harry feel quite small and insignificant.

"I must check it out," Harry said aloud.

Just then, Areeya returned to their station. "How are we doing here, ladies? Is our curry paste ready?"

The three women switched back into cooking mode, setting the gossip aside for the moment.

Sarah held up her blended paste for inspection, "I think we're ready for the next step, Areeya."

The Thai chef smiled approvingly. "Wonderful, let's move on then."

CHAPTER 5

WHALE SHARKS

The sun cast its golden rays onto the cobalt waters around Koh Phangan. Euclid and Connor stood on the deck of a medium-sized center-console diving boat, their feet planted wide apart against the slight roll of the waves beneath them. The boat was a well-equipped, twin-engine vessel designed specifically for diving expeditions. It featured multiple air tanks neatly arranged along the gunwales and a diving platform at the transom for easy access to the water. Snorkels, fins, and masks were stored in mesh containers in the aft cockpit, ready for eager hands to pick up.

"The weather couldn't have been better for this outing," the boat captain told the passengers onboard. "The sea is relatively calm, with just a light breeze. The visibility underwater is as good as it gets. Soon, we will arrive at our diving location, and I hope you'll be able to spot some whale sharks there."

The small group of divers chatted excitedly. Some were asking questions about the various marine species in the area, and others were double-checking their GoPros and underwater cameras. Their anticipation was palpable; for many, whale shark diving was a bucket-list experience, especially around Koh Phangan, where the gentle giants were known to frequent.

"So, have you ever seen a whale shark before?" Connor asked, his eyes gleaming with excitement.

"No, I just finished my PADI training a few weeks ago in Koh Samui," Euclid replied. "But I've always wanted to see one. You?"

"I did my scuba diving course in Bali a few months back, so I'm also quite new to this," Connor replied, grinning. "I went out a few times on trips like this one, but we only ever saw reef sharks. I'm a little anxious right now, so I'm glad I'm not doing it alone."

Euclid nodded, visibly excited. "Man, this is going to be amazing."

"It's quite common to see whale sharks in these waters," Zoë joined in matter-of-factly, putting a damper on Euclid's geeky enthusiasm. She sat next to Connor and Euclid, openly eavesdropping on their conversation. Next to her was the young man whom Euclid met on her arrival at the Hideaway. They exchanged waves, but Grove was busy with his cell phone.

"You must be Zoë, right?" Euclid asked, deciding to ignore her blunt comment. "I saw you talking to my friend, Harry. She said that you guys went to high school together. Small world! Anyway, I'm Euclid, and this here is my new diving pal, Connor."

"Nice to meet you both. Yes, Harry and I grew up in Ithaca, but we were never close friends. It's quite extraordinary to see her here," Zoë answered, her expression unreadable. "By the way, Euclid is quite a rare name. Are your parents mathematicians?"

Euclid, who had been quite accustomed to people asking about his name, confirmed that his father was indeed a professor of mathematics and he himself was teaching Calculus I to freshman engineering students at a university in Seoul.

"Is that where Sarah is from? I spoke to her a little bit at the party," Zoë asked.

"No, Sarah and I are both from Chicago, but we work in Seoul. Sarah was adopted as a baby and is now trying to discover her cultural heritage and learn Korean."

"Oh, and what brings you to Koh Phangan?" Zoë asked Connor.

"I'm here for the diving, obviously," Connor replied, chuckling. "And I suppose a little bit of soul-searching. I work remotely and have found Southeast Asia to be perfect—after a day in front of my laptop, I can walk outside and dive into the ocean or trek across the jungle. And it's not too expensive to live here. How about you? What are you doing here?"

Zoë paused for a moment. "I'm writing a travel blog," she said at last. "I'm exploring the less-known experiences around Thailand, getting the real, local flavor, you know?"

"Just like Harry!" Euclid observed, surprised by the similarities between the two women.

The crew signaled to the divers that they should gather around for the safety briefing. Once the briefing was complete, the boat picked up speed, setting course for what promised to be an unforgettable experience. Euclid couldn't help but feel that the day's adventures would extend beyond just observing the marine life. But for now, the sparkling waters below held enough promise and mystery for everyone on board.

This was a very different scenario than Euclid's last scuba dive—a rescue mission in the dead of night, with the stakes as high as they could ever be. Vivid memories flooded back for a moment. In that pitch-black cave, every move had been calculated. Every second mattered. His torch had pierced through the watery darkness as he searched for the body. The memory of those events had been haunting him, but he decided to shake it off and focus on the here and now.

Today, there were no clouds in the sky, thus allowing the sun to send beams of light dancing through the water and illuminating the marine life below. The dive instructor signaled for the group to level off at around 20 meters, where they'd drift with the current, hoping to encounter the whale sharks that frequented this part of the ocean. Floating there in the deep blue, suspended like an astronaut in space, Euclid felt his thoughts quieten. He looked around, taking in the teeming sea life around him—corals, schools of brightly colored fish, and even a moray eel peeking out from its rocky, marine citadel.

Suddenly, a shadow loomed in the distance, growing steadily larger and more defined. The dive instructor pointed excitedly, and Euclid's heart skipped a beat. It was a whale shark, its massive, polka-dotted body gliding effortlessly through the water, its wide mouth open like a cavern as it sieved plankton from the ocean.

As it swam closer, Euclid could feel his eyes welling up inside his mask. There was something deeply spiritual about sharing the water with a creature so majestic, so ancient. The shark seemed utterly indifferent to the divers, focused solely on its timeless routine of gently drifting and feeding.

Euclid dared to swim a bit closer, always mindful to give the magnificent creature its space. It was a moment of surreal proximity, looking into the eyes of an animal that had been on this Earth far longer than he had. He felt a deep sense of connection, a silent dialogue that transcended species.

The whale shark moved past them, its massive tail propelling it forward with minimal effort. Euclid watched until the magnificent creature became a speck in the distance and eventually disappeared. The dive instructor signaled for the group to ascend, and as they made their way back to the surface, Euclid's heart felt heavy, yet somehow also buoyant, as if lifted by the very ocean that held such wonders.

Once back on the boat, he couldn't help but share glances of awe and excitement with Connor. In that brief underwater moment, all of life's complexities and fear had seemed to vanish, replaced by an overwhelming sense of unity and wonder.

It was an experience that would be etched into his memory forever, something more significant and profound than just a tick on his diving bucket list. As the crew prepared the boat for their return journey, Euclid realized that sometimes the most extraordinary moments were when you came face to face with the vastness of life and found your own place within it. If only he'd known that in the next 24 hours, he would lose the most important person in his life...

A few minutes later, Zoë and Grove also pulled themselves back onto the boat, shedding their dive gear and exchanging exhilarated glances.

"That was incredible," Grove exclaimed, still a little breathless. "I've never experienced anything like that before."

"That's something coming from the heir of one of the biggest wine estates in California," Zoë teased her new friend. "I'd have thought you've seen it all."

"I know. Many people think that, too, but my parents hardly ever leave the vineyard. It's very hands-on," Grove blushed and tried to explain. "It's my first trip abroad on my own."

Connor grinned. "Well, you're in luck then. It was absolutely mind-blowing. Never thought I'd be swimming alongside a giant of the sea."

Zoë, her eyes still shining from the excitement, chimed in, "It's a life-changing experience, isn't it?"

Euclid nodded. "Definitely. Hey, we should all meet for drinks back at the Hideaway to celebrate this unforgettable day."

Zoë laughed. "Sounds like a plan, but don't forget, tonight is one of Reggie's foam parties."

Euclid rolled his eyes at the mention of Reggie's parties. "Ah, yes, the infamous foam party. You can't miss the posters—they're all over the reception area. I even saw a couple in the harbor when we got off the ferry. Not exactly my scene, but—"

"That sounds like fun," Grove interrupted, his interest piqued. "Never been to a foam party before."

"You only live once, right?" Zoë laughed and gave her companion a gentle tap on the shoulder.

"Alright, alright," Euclid conceded with a smile. "Drinks on the deck first, and then we'll see about this foam pool party."

They all nodded in agreement, each privately savoring the thrill of the day's adventure and the anticipation of the night's potential festivities. As the boat headed back toward the Hideaway, their laughter and chatter filled the air, merging with the ocean breeze in a harmonious blend of excitement and camaraderie.

CHAPTER 6

YOU ONLY LIVE ONCE

As the golden rays of the late afternoon sun filtered through the lush greenery surrounding their hut, Sarah and Euclid sat comfortably on their porch, each cradling a refreshing drink. The air was filled with the rustling of the jungle and the chirping of the friendly tokay gecko that watched down upon them from the ceiling.

"So, how was the cooking class?" Euclid asked, his eyes twinkling with genuine curiosity. "Did you finally master the art of the perfect Thai curry?"

Sarah laughed. "Well, let's just say I have a newfound respect for Thai cuisine. It's amazing how they balance so many different flavors and textures. I mean, if teaching English doesn't work out, maybe I should consider a career change."

Euclid chuckled. "From Shakespeare to shrimp curry, quite the transition."

Sarah sipped her drink. "How about you? You looked so pumped this morning heading out for the dive."

Euclid's eyes lit up. "It was incredible, Sarah. Swimming alongside a whale shark was something out of a dream. Their sheer size and the feeling of being so close to such a majestic creature—it was awe-inspiring."

Sarah sensed the passion in his voice. "It sounds like a real Fibonacci sequence of a day, all things aligning perfectly in Nature's grand equation."

Euclid's face broke into an ecstatic grin. While he knew very well that the day was not a Fibonacci sequence in a strict mathematical sense, it made him happy to hear Sarah refer to his great passion. When they first met, Sarah was quite skeptical of the relationship between a literature lover and a mathematician.

"Oh, you have no idea how happy it makes me to hear you say that!" Euclid said.

Sarah smiled softly. "Well, it seems like you were always destined to eat and breathe mathematics. And look at you now, a math teacher diving into the ocean's unknown variables."

"Speaking of the unknown, any updates on Harry's personal quest to find out why the boat her parents were on sank?"

"It's a work in progress it seems. After the cooking class, we walked around the town, and she asked around the port and in some restaurants, but no one seems to know the captain she is looking for. There is a huge language barrier, and many people don't know much English beyond the hospitality phrases. Most of them had no idea what she was talking about and were offering her boat trips. She kept repeating the name, Captain Aroon, hoping it would trigger some memories, but it didn't work. He might have changed his name after the incident. People died when the boat sank, and he spent time in jail for homicide."

"It sounds plausible. I'd change my name, too. Maybe he moved or passed away?"

"We may need to consider that coming here was just chasing a loose end for Harry. But I didn't tell her that. I feel sorry for Harry, but I was also reminded that when we go back to Seoul, I should be more proactive in looking for my biological parents. I really want to know why they abandoned me."

For a moment, they both let the emotional weight of their personal backgrounds hang in the air.

"Well, they say math is the language of the universe. Right now, it's telling me that this moment feels just right."

Their lips met in a tender kiss. A comforting stillness enveloped them as if the universe had graciously granted them this finite moment before life resumed churning out its unpredictable calculations.

As the guests began to pour in for the foam party, I made my way discreetly towards the Hideaway's outbuildings, just behind the reception. The key was already warm from being clenched in my pocket. I quickly unlocked the padlock and slipped inside, closing the door silently behind me. There it was on the top shelf, the contents within marked unmistakably by a yellow triangle and the skull and bones. Ensuring my safety, I donned a face mask and protective glasses before carefully measuring out a teaspoon of the powder.

Why did you have to come here and meddle? I muttered under my breath. With the substance securely sealed in a small bag, I discarded the mask and prepared to blend back into the festivities. *Let's join the party.*

C H A P T E R 7

FOAM POOL
PARTY

H arry locked her hut and paused for a moment. The pulsating bass boom from the foam party vibrated through the air, filling the night. For a moment, she contemplated the idea of skipping the festivities altogether, but then she reasoned that sleep would prove elusive with that level of noise.

Her mind wandered back to her frustrating search for the captain of the boat on which her parents had lost their lives. The trail had gone cold, and the locals didn't seem to have any information about the accident. She had expected a pair of American doctors dying on a boat to have left some traces in the local population's memory. Maybe she was going about this all wrong, she wondered, feeling her heart sink.

Deciding to put her investigation on hold, at least for the night, she took a deep breath. "Time to mix things up a little. Maybe stepping away will bring me a fresh perspective," she murmured to herself, a little unconvinced but still hopeful. "I must drill Zoë more about who the imposter is."

Just as she began to turn toward the sound of the blaring music, she saw Zoë walking briskly toward her.

"Hey, Harry," Zoë said, her eyes glinting mysteriously in the dim light. "Heading to the foam party?"

"Yes, and your timing is impeccable. I was just thinking of you."

"Oh, you know me. I've got a sixth sense for where I'm needed. Let's go."

"Sure, let's go, but only if you tell me who the conman is."

Zoë stopped, and her gaze met Harry's, her eyes searching for any sign of deception. "Keep your voice down, Harry. It's serious. You haven't mentioned this to anyone else? Not even the Korean girl, Sarah, or Euclid?"

Harry shook her head earnestly. "No, Zoë, I swear, I haven't said a word to anyone."

Nodding, Zoë lowered her voice to a whisper. "I'm trailing someone who's swindled millions from wealthy socialites in California and across the U.S."

Her curiosity piqued, Harry couldn't help but ask, "But who is it?"

Zoë rolled her eyes and sighed. "I can't risk compromising my story. You'll find out at the Full Moon Party. Tomorrow, we can discuss the details of my trap. What I can say is this: Be careful. Not everyone at Mango Moon Hideaway is who they say they are. There's a snake among us, ready to strike when least expected."

A shiver ran down Harry's spine as she took in the warning. Could there really be someone with sinister motives mingling among them, or was Zoë exaggerating for the sake of her story?

"Let's not talk about it anymore," Zoë said, abruptly interrupting Harry's train of thought. "The walls of these coconut huts are paper-thin. Someone could easily eavesdrop."

Nodding her agreement, Harry let the subject drop, although a sense of foreboding didn't leave her entirely. Together, they made their way to the pool area, the thumping bassline drawing them closer.

As they joined the party, Harry couldn't help but wonder who the 'snake' might be. But for now, the foam, the lights, and the pulsating music filled the air, creating an atmosphere too engrossing to resist. Maybe, just for tonight, she could forget her worries and lose herself in the moment.

A DJ was spinning some of the hottest tracks, and columns of foam burst from machines at the corners of the pool, creating a frothy wonderland where people laughed, danced, and splashed about.

Harry, Sarah, Euclid, and Connor chatted and sipped their drinks. Their faces were animated under the colorful disco lights. They saw Somchai and Reggie, trays with cocktails in hand, mingling with the guests, chatting and offering welcome drinks. Reggie sauntered over to their group. He was carrying a tray of elaborately garnished cocktails that seemed almost too beautiful to drink.

"Ah, my wonderful guests! How are you enjoying the foam-tastic evening?" Reggie boomed, his voice full of exuberance. "I've got something special for you all—some of our signature Thai cocktails. This one is called the 'Siam Sunray', a delightful blend of vodka, coconut milk, and a touch of chili. And this one, my friends, is the 'Bangkok Breeze', a concoction of gin, lemongrass, and kaffir lime leaves."

Intrigued and grateful, they each took a cocktail from the tray. The drinks were as delicious as they were beautiful, capturing the essence of Thai flavors in each sip.

Euclid looked around at the large crowd and then back at Reggie. "This is quite the turnout. Are all these people guests at Mango Moon?"

Reggie chuckled. "Oh, you'd be surprised! My foam parties have become something of a local legend. Many of these folks come from neighboring resorts just to join in on the fun. I like to think of it as an appetizer to the grand feast that is the Full Moon Party. I usually host one of these events a few days before the big event."

Sarah took a sip of her cocktail and then faced Reggie, curiosity twinkling in her eyes. "So, is it true you were on an Australian reality show?"

Reggie's eyes lit up at the question as if he'd been waiting for someone to ask him it all evening. He straightened his back, puffed out his chest, adjusted his ascot, and smiled broadly. Harry wondered how he was able to wear so many layers of formal attire in the humid Thai climate, but then, gentlemen's clothing was never within the scope of her interests. It was his choice if Reggie wanted to look smart by wearing long sleeves and ascots.

"Ah, so you've heard of my little stint Down Under, have you? It wasn't just any reality show, my dear. It was *Australia's Ultimate Tycoon*, a competition for the brightest business minds and the savviest entrepreneurs. Imagine the drama of *Survivor* with the complexity of *Shark Tank*, but multiplied by ten, and you might just begin to understand the competition. I had to beat some of the toughest, smartest businesspeople from around the world. At the end of it, I was something of a folk hero. They called me 'The Magician of Market Strategy'. I was offered several TV deals after the show, but I chose to invest in Mango Moon Hideaway. Far more fulfilling, don't you think?"

"That is an incredible story, Reggie. So, is it true you are also a writer?" Harry could see that her friend was probably an excellent teacher, listening intently and always ready with follow-up questions.

Reggie took a moment, as if searching for the right words, and then replied enigmatically, "Ah, the realms of storytelling. A beautiful, endless frontier, much like the mind itself. But you see, my relationship with writing is somewhat... unconventional. One might even say I've dabbled in the alchemy of words, weaving narratives that touch on the edges of reality. But to label me as a mere 'writer' would be to confine the boundless nature of expression. I prefer to think of myself as a storyteller, a shaper of worlds, if you will."

The word salad left Harry somewhat perplexed. Reggie's response didn't exactly confirm or deny his supposed literary background. It merely added another layer to his enigmatic personality, leaving her to ponder just how much of what he said could be believed.

"That's enough about me, darlings. I hope you have a fabulous evening. I'll remind Somchai to bring you another round of cocktails. On the house, of course."

As they watched Reggie walk away to entertain other guests, Connor shook his head, chuckling. "That guy's quite a character."

Euclid nodded. "You can say that again. He's like a novel that never ends."

Sarah then piped up, a grin forming on her lips. "You guys have no idea. There are so many stories about Reginald Winthorpe, or 'Reggie', as he likes to call himself. I mean, it's hard to keep track."

Harry sighed. "It's also hard to tell with him what's true and what's not."

Euclid picked up his drink, savoring another sip. "One thing's for sure: Reggie knows how to be a generous host. These cocktails are seriously strong."

Sarah set hers down. "Well, I'm going to take advantage of these strong cocktails and hit the dance floor."

Harry shook her head. "I think I'll pass on dancing tonight."

Euclid and Connor glanced at each other. "How about we get some whiskey shots? We've got some whale shark tales to swap," Euclid suggested.

Connor nodded, and the two headed toward the bar, leaving Sarah to her dancing and Harry to her thoughts.

It was late into the night when Harry finally decided she'd had enough. The music was still thumping, and the crowd was still buzzing, but she felt drained. She said her goodbyes and made her way back to her cabin, her mind still swirling with the enigma that was Reggie, the strong cocktails, and the looming questions about her own quest. The door to her cabin closed behind her with a soft click, shutting some of the noise out and leaving her to the solitude of her thoughts.

CHAPTER 8

GONE

In the murky haze of sleep, Harry found herself trapped in a recurring dream. She had been standing on a rickety boat, her feet unsteady on the swaying deck. Dark storm clouds loomed overhead, and turbulent waves crashed against the hull. Her parents were there too, their faces filled with fear. Her mother reached out, almost touching her, when a towering wave rose like a monstrous wall, eclipsing everything. A feeling of dread came over Harry's body as she stared into the foaming sea, watching her mother get dragged away by the storm and start to sink.

"Do something!" she shouted, turning to where her father was standing, but he wasn't there anymore. As she looked back, her mother was gone, too, lost in the dark waters of the ferocious storm around them. While Harry had no idea if this was how her parents had died, the dream embodied the enormous sadness and grief that she carried for their loss.

Just as another wave was about to crash down, a piercing scream shattered the nightmare. Harry jolted awake, her heart pounding. She wiped a few stray tears from her cheek and looked around. Momentarily disoriented, she struggled to separate the dream from reality. Then she realized where she was—in her hut at Mango Moon Hideaway—and felt a wave of relief wash over her. The boat, the storm, her parents—they had all been fragments of a haunting dream.

But then it hit her. The scream wasn't part of the dream; it was real and had echoed through the jungle outside her hut.

Alarmed, Harry quickly threw on a pair of shorts and a T-shirt. She unlocked her door and stepped out into the pre-dawn light, her senses sharpened, her mind still echoing with that chilling scream. Something was wrong, very wrong.

Harry rushed toward where she thought the scream had come from, her heart pounding in her chest. The sound seemed to have originated from the pool area. As she passed by Euclid and Sarah's hut, she noticed Euclid sleeping in the hammock on the porch. She shook him awake, and he groaned, clearly having ended his night of revelry only a few hours earlier.

"Euclid, did you hear that scream?" Harry asked, urgency lacing her voice.

He rubbed his eyes and looked around. "What? No, I didn't hear anything. What's going on?"

"I heard a horrifying scream. Something's wrong. Come with me," Harry insisted.

Euclid groaned lazily but reluctantly swung his legs over the side of the hammock. "Alright, but after we figure this out, I'm going back to bed. It's probably a bird or a wild animal in the jungle."

Harry hesitated, considering the possibility. Euclid had made a good point. Perhaps the scream had seemed more terrifying because she heard it while experiencing a nightmare. It could have been just a pair of wild cats cavorting in the early hours. But since she was now outside and had woken Euclid, she decided to continue with her initial impulse to find the source of the sound.

They hurried toward the pool area, and the scene that greeted them was the aftermath of a wild party. Patches of foam were scattered everywhere, empty glasses littered the tables and poolside, and the air smelled strongly of alcohol and chlorine. Some people who had been sleeping on sun loungers were now sitting up, looking just as disoriented as Euclid had been, clearly awakened by the scream Harry had heard.

Upon seeing a distressed staff member on the other side of the pool, Harry felt a jolt of adrenaline. The cleaner stood helpless amidst the foam covering most of the floor and some of the furnishings surrounding the pool. Her mop was on the ground, and she was trying to dial a number on her phone, but her hands were slippery and shaking. As she saw Harry and Euclid approach, she spoke frantically in broken English.

"Mam, sir, don't come. She dead."

Harry shook her head, unable to understand. The woman put her hand forward to stop Harry and stammered, "Dead... I call police..."

Harry's veins turned to ice as she looked past the cleaner and saw Zoë's face. Surrounded by puffs of delicate white foam, the visage would have been peaceful, almost angelic, but the fixed grimace of her mouth and the bluish tint of her lips told Harry that Zoë was gone. It was a macabre tableau, one that would be etched in her memory forever. Harry turned around and gestured to Euclid for him to stay where he was before he came any closer and saw the dead body.

"Who is it?" Euclid asked.

"It's Zoë. It looks like she's dead," Harry whispered, almost afraid to say the words out loud.

The cleaner was now crying hysterically, unable to control herself. Faced with the unraveling drama, Harry attempted to stay strong. She pulled the cleaner away from the body and tried to comfort her as she got her to sit down on a nearby chair. Harry felt paralyzed, unsure of what action to take.

"Euclid, tell the others to stay away. We need to protect the scene so the police can investigate."

Euclid nodded. "On it. But what happened? Was there an accident?" he asked in apprehension.

"I really don't know," Harry said while stroking the head of the sobbing woman. "Her face is blue. It looks like she drowned or suffocated. It's awful. Don't look."

Just then, Somchai appeared, wearing a bathrobe over her nightdress and looking as bewildered as everyone else. The cleaner stood up and started rapidly conversing with her in Thai, causing Somchai's face to become visibly distressed. She quickly pulled a cell phone from her pocket and dialed a number, her fingers trembling as she tapped the screen.

"One of our guests is dead," she said to the person on the other end of the line, her voice shaky. "The cleaner, Mai, found her by the pool. You need to come here soon. The police are on the way."

Somchai pocketed her phone and turned to Harry and Euclid, her face a mask of grim solemnity.

"Reggie will get here as soon as he can. It seems he went with some of the guests to another resort."

A profound sense of doom settled over Harry. Zoë had warned her not to trust anyone at Mango Moon Hideaway.

"Are we sure she's actually dead?" Euclid asked, gripping the edge of a pool chair to steady himself.

"I'm sure," Harry responded with certainty. "Her face is blue. Her eyes are wide open, Euclid."

"Shouldn't we try to check her pulse?"

"Euclid, I worked as a reporter for my local newspaper in Ithaca. Every summer, people drown in Cayuga Lake. I have seen post-mortem photos of some of the victims. I even shadowed a coroner so I could understand their job. I've seen this facial expression before. When you fight for your last breath of air, your mouth gets fixed in this contorted grimace. It's horrific."

The revelation hung in the air, a stark contrast to the remnants of the previous night's party surrounding them. The foam, the empty glasses, and the disheveled loungers now took on a darker, more sinister hue as they all absorbed the reality of the tragedy that had just unfolded.

Euclid considered Harry's words. "But how would she drown? She's lying on the floor next to the pool. Can someone drown in foam?"

Somchai shook her head. "I have no idea. I'm sure the police will be able to determine the cause of death."

Euclid glanced around. "If there's foul play, collecting evidence here will be next to impossible anyway. Look at this place."

Somchai nodded in agreement. "Please don't even say that. It must have been some sort of an accident. Maybe she took some drugs or drank too much. Did you know her?"

Before Harry could answer, some of the guests who had blacked out on the sun loungers started to stir, overhearing their grim conversation. They looked around, disoriented, then began to make their way toward the exit.

"Please, stay where you are and don't leave the Hideaway," Somchai called out to them. "The police are on their way, and it's important no one leaves the scene."

Collective tension filled the air as reality sank in. They were all now part of a terrible tragedy, one that had turned their tropical paradise into a crime scene. On hearing the sound of sirens, Somchai took charge of the small crowd of guests and directed everyone, including Harry and Euclid, to the reception area. She instructed them to remain there until the police spoke to them. Somchai then went outside to await the arrival of the police.

Sitting on the comfortable puffs and bean bags in the open-air reception, Harry observed the party-goers, whose epic adventure had turned into a nightmare. Still trying to process what she had just seen, she overheard shreds of conversations, mostly unfounded rumors about who the victim might be and what might have happened. After what seemed like an eternity, a stern-looking Thai man in civilian clothes appeared and asked if anyone at the resort could identify the body. He took off his mirrored aviators and introduced himself as

Detective Niran. His medium-length dark hair, styled with a lot of gel, made him look like a member of a boyband, but his demeanor and body language were far from frivolous.

Harry hesitated momentarily, wrestling with her concerns that revealing her acquaintance with Zoë might put her in the crosshairs of whoever Zoë had been investigating. Ultimately, her sense of decency won out. It didn't feel right to let Zoë be taken away without someone familiar acknowledging her passing.

"I knew her in New York," Harry said, raising her hand. "Her name is... *was* Zoë Kessler."

His eyes narrowed, scrutinizing her. "Please follow me. Everyone else, please stay where you are. An officer is on her way to take your statements on what you can remember from last night. If you can remember anything..." He gave the hungover group of young people a judgmental look.

Harry didn't think it was necessary to go back to the body to identify it officially but decided not to argue with the detective. She asked if Euclid could come with her for moral support, and the detective agreed. Once Harry had confirmed that it was Zoë who was deceased, she stepped away from the body.

"So, you came here together on holiday, right?" the detective asked, busy taking notes.

"No, we just met here by chance," Harry explained.

"That's a strange coincidence. What was she doing here?"

"I'm not sure," Harry said, electing not to reveal Zoë's secret investigation. "She's an influencer—a travel blogger. You can find her on Instagram and other social media."

The detective wrote down the profile names.

"Well, we will try to contact her family in Ithaca, and we need you to stay here until we clear this up. I need you to come to the police station for a formal interview. I'll send someone over as soon as we collect all the evidence."

"Yes, of course," Harry said. Worried that she was making a huge mistake by not mentioning Zoë's real assignment, she paused and gathered some courage to ask the question that had been bothering her since she had first seen Zoë's body. "Do you think someone killed her?"

"Look, Ms. Sinclair. I can't tell you much, but since you knew each other in the past and you might be the main point of contact for her family in the States, it looks to me like a tragic accident. It appears that she suffocated somehow. My best guess is that she drowned."

"Drowned? But how?" Euclid inquired. "Perhaps she was choked to death?"

"If she had been strangled, there would be marks on her neck," the detective answered patiently. "I could see plainly, even without the autopsy, that there was no bruising."

"But if she drowned in the swimming pool, why was she lying on the ground by the pool?" Harry asked.

"Unfortunately, there are many ways to drown," Somchai spoke up solemnly. "Many people have never heard of secondary drowning, but it's a silent killer."

Both she and Euclid shook their heads.

"She's right," the detective explained. "Secondary drowning can happen when you are not in the water. We see it occasionally on the island, with all the water sports and water activities that visitors do. It's rare, but it happens. Based on her facial expression and the lack of any visible attack marks on her body, I suspect that is what happened. It occurs when a small amount of water gets trapped in your lungs, causing swelling and inflammation. The person usually suffocates hours after the initial incident. Was she doing any water sports before the party?"

"Actually, I was with her and some other guests yesterday," Euclid said. "We were scuba diving and swimming with sharks."

The detective wrote the information down, nodding.

"That makes sense. We will also run some toxicology tests to see if she was taking any drugs that might have caused her death. But secondary drowning remains my informed guess."

The detective stopped talking as the black body bag was wheeled into the ambulance.

"Anyway, I have your details, and I will be in touch very soon to get your official statements," the detective said before walking briskly towards the reception area.

Once he was out of earshot, Harry turned to Euclid. "Do you think he suspects me?"

"I think he thinks it's strange how you and Zoë ended here, so far away from home," Euclid replied. "I'm quite sure people lie to him all the time, so he's suspicious by nature. It's his job."

Hearing Euclid's words, Harry felt embarrassed and worried. She had indeed lied to the well-spoken Detective Niran when she failed to disclose Zoë's real purpose for being at the Hideaway and the fact that Zoë wrote to her and asked for her help to catch a fraudster. She felt terrible for withholding information from the police and not being honest with Euclid.

They walked in silence toward Euclid's hut; Harry was worried about the consequences of lying to the police, and Euclid was emotionally exhausted. He had never seen a dead body or dealt with an accidental death. His typical day had a fixed routine of getting up, going for a jog, and then drinking coffee with his girlfriend while they both prepared for their classes at the university. How he now missed the predictability of it all! The small joys of a simple life.

Finally, Harry broke the quiet moment. "I think I know why she was killed."

Euclid looked at Harry, visibly shocked. "What? I thought she drowned," he whispered. "What do you mean she was killed?"

"I didn't tell the police because Zoë swore me to secrecy," Harry explained. "But there was more to Zoë than being a social media influencer. She told me something that makes sense now. There's a conman at the Hideaway, a swindler. Zoë was writing a story about them, but she never managed to tell me who they were."

"Okay, Harry, this is too much for me for one morning," Euclid said, stopping her. "I need to gather my thoughts. I really need some caffeine to process all of this," he continued, rubbing his temples. "And I need to wake Sarah up. I can't believe she's slept through the police sirens and all the commotion outside. Let's reconvene at lunchtime."

"Good idea," Harry agreed. "I'll start up my laptop and find Zoë's parents—they're probably on Facebook. I'll write to my grandmother to tell her what has happened. Perhaps she can go over to their house and tell them in person."

Euclid entered his hut, but Harry remained on the path for a few minutes, taking in deep breaths and trying to calm herself down. She was about to head to her own hut when she suddenly heard her name being called out. Euclid re-emerged onto the porch of his bamboo accommodation. His face was grey, drained of color.

"What's happened?" Harry gasped, her heart pounding in her chest.

Euclid looked at her with wide, panicked eyes. "Sarah's gone, and she's not answering her phone."

There was no time to waste.

"We need to talk to the police before they go. Hurry!"

CHAPTER 9

THE SEARCH BEGINS

E uclid and Harry hurried back to the reception area, where Detective Niran was talking to Reggie and Somchai. One of the constables was still taking statements from the partygoers, but the crowd was much smaller than before. Seeing the detective, Euclid approached with a sense of urgency.

"I'm sorry to interrupt," he began, addressing Somchai. "I can't find Sarah. She's missing, and she didn't sleep in our hut last night."

Somchai's eyes widened, visibly alarmed.

"She's my girlfriend; I can't find her," Euclid then explained to the detective.

The detective adjusted his sunglasses on the top of his head and closed his notebook.

"Maybe your girlfriend found herself another boyfriend?" he said, with a dismissive wave of his hand. "Look, my friend. Koh Phangan is a party island. Young people come here to have fun. Sometimes, they break each other's hearts. It really is not a matter for the police."

Euclid clenched his fists, struggling to contain his frustration. "This isn't a joke. She wouldn't just go off without telling me. Something is seriously wrong. I've called her dozens of times, and she isn't answering her phone."

The detective shrugged, his impassive face unchanging. "We see a lot of drama on the island. People drink too much and let their emotions guide them. I'm sure she'll call you back as soon as she wakes up... wherever she is."

Euclid was on the brink of tears as he desperately tried to convey to the detective that his girlfriend wouldn't just run away. "You don't understand; something terrible must have happened to her," he insisted, his voice shaky.

Harry chimed in to support Euclid, emphasizing how close he and Sarah were as a couple. "They are practically inseparable. Something isn't right."

The detective, however, remained unswayed by their emotional appeals.

At that moment, Reggie decided to intervene. "Look, before we jump to any conclusions, let's do a thorough search of Mango Moon Hideaway. She might still be here somewhere. Maybe she fell asleep on the beach. It wouldn't be the first time that's happened."

Somchai spoke in Thai, clearly making the case for the young couple, and the detective reluctantly nodded. "Fine," he said, signaling to some of his men who were around the pool area helping collect evidence. "We will search all the huts and the beach. But let's do it quickly."

The detective beckoned two police officers to come closer, briefly conferring with them in rapid Thai before turning his attention back to Euclid. "Describe her," he demanded curtly.

Euclid swallowed hard, trying to gather his thoughts. "She has long black hair, green eyes..." He paused, realizing it would be more efficient to show a picture. Pulling out his phone, he quickly found a recent photo of Sarah and presented it to the detective.

"Her nationality?" the detective questioned, studying the image closely.

"She's Korean American," Euclid responded.

Nodding, the detective gestured for Euclid to send him a copy of the photo. Once it arrived on his device, he quickly shared it with the two waiting officers.

"And what was she wearing last night?" he continued to probe.

Euclid hesitated, attempting to recollect. "I think... a dress?"

Harry, who stood a few steps away, interjected, "No, she had on green shorts and a red tank top."

The detective took note of the details and relayed the description to the two officers in Thai, who promptly set off to begin their search. He then gestured towards Euclid's hut. "Come with me," he commanded. "I wish to search your accommodation personally."

Though obviously anxious, Euclid nodded, then turned to Somchai, his face pale and etched with worry. "Somchai, could you come with us? We might need your help—you know this place inside-out."

Reggie, overhearing the conversation, chimed in, "While you all sort that out, I need to go around the resort. We must calm everyone down and stop the gossip before it gets out of hand."

Harry trailed behind as the group made their way to Euclid's hut, her thoughts swirling with concern for Sarah. The detective led the way, and once they arrived, he signaled for them to wait outside as he entered.

Euclid sat down on the steps to his hut's porch, the seriousness of the situation evident in his defeated posture. He rubbed his temples. "I shouldn't have been drinking with Connor last night," he murmured, his voice cracking with emotion. "We just... we got lost in the moment, and I can't even remember how or when I got back to the hut."

He paused, taking a shaky breath. "The last thing I remember was the beauty and warmth of the tropical night. I thought the hammock on the porch was a good place to sleep off the alcohol. I should've checked if Sarah was inside, but I was sure she was sleeping and didn't want to disturb her."

Somchai placed a gentle hand on his arm. "Euclid, this isn't your fault. You couldn't have known this would happen. Now, we need to focus on finding Sarah. It's possible she just fell asleep on the beach."

Euclid's emotions got the better of him, and tears began to flow. Somchai sat with him, offering a silent, comforting presence.

The detective emerged from the hut, his expression unreadable. He announced that he found nothing of consequence inside. Turning to Somchai, he instructed, "Lock the hut. Don't let anyone inside in case this becomes a..." He hesitated, unwilling to say the word *murder* in front of a distraught Euclid, and settled for "... another investigation."

"Let's wait in the cafeteria," Somchai suggested. We could all use some strong coffee right now." As the detective began to walk away, taking note of other areas of interest, Connor appeared on the path in front of the hut, looking confused and concerned.

"I've just been woken up by the police searching for Sarah. What's going on?" he asked, his voice laden with sleep and confusion.

Harry took a deep breath and gave him a brief rundown of the morning's harrowing events—from discovering Zoë's lifeless body to Sarah's unexplained disappearance.

Connor's face paled. "I can't believe this," he muttered, clearly struggling to process the information. When I last saw them, they were both on the dance floor, having fun in the foam with the other guests. To be honest, that's all I remember. I don't even recall getting to my hut. The whiskey here is very strong."

"You should all wait at the reception area or the cafeteria. I'll go with the detective to the beach and let you know if they find anything," Somchai advised them.

"I'm coming with you," Euclid announced and followed her and the policeman.

"The two of you can stay here," the detective stopped Harry before she offered to come with them. "I don't need that many footprints on the beach... just in case."

As the group headed off, Harry's gaze caught a glimpse of a bright pink object sitting conspicuously on the porch table. A sense of recognition washed over her. Harry couldn't remember if the object was there when they first approached the hut, but the significance of the item wasn't lost on her. It was Zoë's pink vape pen. A flurry of questions raced through her mind: Had Zoë been vaping outside Euclid's hut that night? If not, who had placed it there? And for what reason? Was someone attempting to implicate Euclid in Zoë's death?

Trusting her instincts, Harry discreetly walked past the table. Without drawing attention, she grabbed the vape pen and slipped it into her pocket. She fervently hoped that she had made the right move.

CHAPTER 10

THE VOW

Connor and Harry sat in the Hideaway's restaurant, their table perfectly positioned to give them an unobstructed sea view. The vast expanse of blue water now appeared threatening as dark clouds amassed above, turning the once serene water into a churning, restless expanse.

A waitress carrying a tray holding steaming cups of coffee walked over to their table and set their drinks down. "It'll rain soon," she remarked, nodding towards the looming clouds. "Monsoon season. Best to stay indoors." With that, she walked away, leaving the pair to their thoughts.

Connor filled the silence by chatting about trivial matters, but Harry barely registered his words. Her mind was racing, trying to piece together the events that had unfolded so suddenly. The image of Zoë's face haunted her. Though they weren't close friends, their shared profession in the demanding world of New York journalism had forged a tentative bond of understanding and mutual respect.

Lost in thought, Harry made a silent vow: she would get to the bottom of what had happened to Zoë. For closure, for justice, and for the bond that every journalist working in the field share. The storm brewing outside was symbolic of the tempest that raged in her heart. As the first drops of rain began to fall, Harry felt a renewed determination to uncover the truth.

"*Mon Dieu!* Such terrible news this morning, *non*?" Harry's dark thoughts were interrupted by Pierre. Dominique trailed just behind him, looking distraught.

"It's horrible!" Dominique said. "We are so, so sorry about Zoë. And Sarah... *Mon Dieu!* Euclid must be very upset, no?"

Harry nodded. "He's with the police searching the beach."

"The police, do they have any clues?" Pierre asked, trying to make sense of it all.

Harry shook her head. "Not yet. They're still investigating."

Dominique waved over a waitress. "Two coffees, please," she requested and then turned back to the group, her eyes searching each face. "This island was supposed to be a paradise, but now, it feels more like a... nightmare."

"*Oui*, a *réal cauchemar*," Pierre agreed, sighing heavily. They both settled into the chairs, their expressions mirroring the somber mood at the table.

"We knew nothing about this until just now," Dominique said, breaking the uncomfortable silence. "Pierre and I... we went for a long hike before dawn. We love to watch the sunrise from the mountains. When we returned, it was chaos: police everywhere, and so many people on the beach."

"I'm sure it will be okay," Connor said, sipping his coffee. "Sarah might have gone for a long walk along the beach. I can't imagine why else she would disappear..."

"I'm not sure, Connor," Harry wasn't so optimistic. "I can't imagine she would be gone for that long. Also, don't forget that we had quite a few cocktails last night. Somchai and Reggie were serving them all night. I don't think she'd be in the mood for a long walk."

As if on cue, a sudden clamor from the beach down below disrupted their conversation. A loud noise, shouts, and what sounded like the frantic movement of people echoed up to the restaurant. Harry stood up abruptly, knocking over her chair. "They might've found her," she whispered.

Without another word, she dashed off in the direction of the noise, down the narrow path leading from the restaurant to the beach. Connor followed suit. Dominique and Pierre exchanged glances before they, too, stood up to find out what had caused the uproar, their coffees forgotten.

As Harry and Connor neared the small search party, the policemen and some Hideaway staff stepped aside, revealing Detective Niran and Euclid. The detective carefully held up an evidence bag with what looked like a smartphone inside.

"Is this Sarah's?" he inquired, holding it out for Euclid to see.

Euclid's voice trembled as he responded, "Yes, that's hers. It looks like hers. It's the same turquoise case. Have you found her? Where is she?"

The detective shook his head, a matter-of-fact expression on his face. "No, we haven't found her. One of the volunteers discovered the phone half buried in the sand," he explained. "Do you know the passcode to unlock it?"

Euclid nodded eagerly and opened the phone to find several unread messages and missed call notifications. They were all from him. He passed the cell phone to the detective, who wrote down the passcode for future access.

"It's not much use to us since we are standing in the last place where Sarah might have used it. So, where could she have gone from here? Did someone take her and then throw away her phone? Did she go on a boat to another resort?"

The detective glanced down at the chaotic prints dotting the beach. "There are far too many footprints to identify any specific tracks or suspects."

Harry's attention was drawn to a cluster of small boats moored a short distance away. She pointed to them, curiosity evident in her voice. "Whose boats are those?"

"They belong to the local fishermen," the detective answered, following her gaze. "We intend to interview the owners. Perhaps they saw something in the early hours of the morning before they set off fishing."

Soon, Connor, Dominique, and Pierre joined the policemen. As Euclid updated them on his findings, the detective's eyes met Harry's, his intent clear. He gestured discreetly for her to step away from the crowd. It was evident he had more to discuss with her, and he wanted to do it privately. Harry complied, her journalistic instincts alert and ready.

The detective looked earnestly at Harry. "I need to ask some sensitive questions, and I didn't want to do it in front of Sarah's boyfriend," he began, hesitating for a moment before continuing. "Do you think there's any chance that Sarah might have been... suicidal?"

Harry blinked rapidly, taken aback. The question hung in the air between them. She thought of Sarah's sweet smiling face, the way she laughed, and the vibrant energy she always exuded. But Harry also knew that outward appearances could be deceiving. The mind was a complex thing; even the brightest of smiles can hide the darkest of personalities.

"I... I don't know her well enough to say," Harry admitted. "She always appeared happy and lively, but then, I wasn't close to her, personally. Maybe her family in Chicago would have better insight into her state of mind."

The detective nodded slowly. "Do you think it's possible she might have... drowned herself?"

"It's hard to imagine," she responded. "She seemed very happy yesterday, joking with everyone, drinking cocktails, and dancing, but then, we never truly know what someone is going through."

The detective's gaze was fixed on the horizon. "At the moment, given the lack of evidence or clues pointing elsewhere, we have to consider every possibility, including suicide," he said with a heavy sigh. "I'm going to bring more officers to search the area—both the beach and the surrounding jungle. I think we need to call the search and rescue team from Surat Thani to bring the dogs; otherwise, it's like looking for a needle in a haystack. In the meantime, keep me informed if you hear any information about last night that might shed more light on what happened to these two women. Here's my number."

Harry took Detective Niran's card and nodded. The uncertainty was agonizing, but jumping to conclusions could also be dangerous. It was crucial to keep an open mind.

Pierre quickly intercepted Harry as she moved away. "Harry, what did the detective say?" he asked. "Has he got any suspects?"

Harry hesitated momentarily, deciding not to share the detective's thoughts on the matter. "They're going to extend the investigation and bring more officers and search and rescue dogs to help look for her, Pierre," she replied.

Pierre sighed. "All this... it's incredibly distressing. When I feel overwhelmed, I find hiking to be therapeutic. Clears the mind," he said, pausing before continuing. "If you like, we could go for a hike to Khao Ra tomorrow. It's the highest peak on Koh Phangan. The views from there are breathtaking, and they will help clear your head."

Harry looked at Pierre, contemplating his offer. With all the chaos, the idea of a break sounded appealing, even if just for a few hours. However, she remembered her physical limitations. "I'm not the best hiker, Pierre. I have fibromyalgia, and sometimes it acts up, especially during stressful times," she explained, a hint of reluctance in her voice.

Pierre nodded understandingly. "I promise we'll go at your pace. Nature has a way of healing, even if we're just spending time surrounded by it."

Harry considered his suggestion for a moment longer and then agreed. "Alright, but you'll have to bear with me. First thing tomorrow morning, then?"

Pierre smiled. "Bright and early. It will be good for us."

It was late afternoon when Harry finally found herself alone on her porch. The sprawling jungle before her seemed more active than ever, swarming with life. The cacophony of sound from the thick forest was both eerie and comforting. She could hear the distant, wailing hoots of gibbons, their calls banefully communicating a coded message from one end of the jungle to another. The rhythmic croaking of slimy jungle frogs provided a beating bassline to the tropical chorus, celebrating the recent rain that had rejuvenated their spirits. A series of sharp, crisp chirps sounded from the undergrowth—perhaps a gecko or some other nocturnal creature stirring to life. Every now and then, the shrill, panicked call of a fat cicada would pierce the air, instantly breaking Harry's chain of thought.

The air was thick with humidity, making her skin feel slightly clammy. Rain droplets lazily dripped from the leaves above, their wet patter a reminder of the heavy downpour earlier. Harry thought of the evidence lost with every drop of water that fell—the footprints and potential clues that the rain might have erased. A part of her felt immense, pitiful sadness for Sarah's parents. She was their most precious possession, a little girl adopted in their late thirties after a fruitless decade of trying to conceive a baby. Harry could not imagine the heartache of the unknown, the pain Sarah's parents would feel, and the weight of the blame they would, perhaps unfairly, place on Euclid.

The recent rain had also left a fresh, earthy scent in the air. Harry took a deep breath of its pungency, attempting to ground herself amidst the turmoil she felt in her soul. She needed clarity, and perhaps the very heart of nature, pulsating with life around her, could provide some insight into the chaotic tapestry of complex human life she found herself entangled in.

The puff of a gentle breeze carried the fleeting scent of freshly bloomed flowers, triggering a lucid memory from Harry's past. She was a child again, enveloped by the familiar warmth of her grandparents' home. The conservative yellow wallpaper, the smell of charred wood mixed with freshly baked cinnamon rolls from the homestead oven, and recollection of the comforting creak of wooden floorboards all embraced her in comforting nostalgia.

She saw her younger self, her hair tied back in two symmetrical braids, lying on her stomach on a red and green checkered blanket. She was in the middle of her Nancy Drew mystery. There was a whole box set of the series on the bookcase next to her bed. The bedroom where she used to sleep was once her mom's, and while her grandparents had updated the wallpaper and changed some furniture to suit their granddaughter's taste, they left her mother's collection of books for Harry to enjoy whenever she came to stay with them.

Nancy Drew was about to open a secret door in an abandoned house when the electric chime of the doorbell downstairs disrupted Harry's reading. Being the curious child she was, she left her book on her pillow and tiptoed out onto the upstairs landing. She squatted down, peering through the wooden balusters of the staircase, trying to catch a glimpse of who was at the door. The words from below were muffled, disjointed phrases rising and falling away, making it impossible for her to piece together the conversation. But the tone—heavy and grim—told her something terrible had happened.

A profound silence settled over the house when the front door finally closed behind the unexpected visitor. It wasn't the quiet peace of her grandmother taking an afternoon nap or the lull in household chores on a lazy summer's day. It was a sterile silence, laden with grief—thick and suffocating.

Hours seemed to pass before her grandmother's gentle footsteps approached her room. The look on her face was one Harry would never forget. It was one that preceded the devastating news that her parents, her proud pillars of strength and love, were no longer of this world. The enormity of that truth, a reality too cruel for such a young, innocent child to comprehend, pressed down on her chest, making it hard to breathe. The memory of that hurtful day remained etched in her mind, a scar that time could never fully heal.

The golden hour cast long shadows on the porch. Harry's mind was filled with memories. Her dear grandmother's soft voice echoed in her ears, "They're gone, sweetheart." Even as a child, Harry had noticed the deliberate avoidance of the word *dead*. It was as though her grandmother believed its absence could somehow soften the blow or, perhaps, keep a glimmer of hope alive. But as she uttered the painful words, her grandmother could not hold back the tears. They lay cuddled on the bed in her mother's old bedroom for hours, crying quietly. Grieving not for what had happened but for what would never happen; both the grandmother and her granddaughter had been robbed of memories that were meant to be.

Harry drew a deep breath, the wetness of plump tears forming at the corner of her eyes. The raw ache of not being able to offer a final goodbye was overwhelming. "I just need closure," she whispered in desperation. "I need to say my last goodbye."

The urgent matters of the present snapped her back to reality. She must find Sarah and figure out what had happened to Zoë. Did she really drown? To clear her overwrought conscience, Harry had to find out who Zoë was investigating. This would answer the question of whether her death was accidental or not. Who was the 'snake', as Zoë had called them? Who was not what they appeared to be? These tasks loomed large, forcing Harry to channel her pain into steely determination. The past was agonizing, but the present demanded her complete focus, and she was resolved to find answers.

C H A P T E R 11

ON LAND

Twelve hours earlier, as the first rays of sunlight splashed across the sky in soft hues of pastel pink and orange, Sarah and two other Thai women were pulled ashore by rough hands. Not far from the beach, the distant outline of a quaint village was visible. Sarah's hands trembled, and a piercing headache throbbed behind her eyes—the cruel combination of a hangover, petrol fumes, and rising panic. Frantically, she patted down the pockets of her shorts, but her cell phone was nowhere to be found. *How did she end up here? Did they kidnap her at the foam party? Surely, she'd have remembered being taken?*

Recent stories echoed in her mind, like the chilling incident of a foreign tourist's abduction near the Thai-Malay border, supposedly by separatist groups who were rebelling against the Thai government. Fearing her American identity might turn her into a valuable hostage, Sarah decided to hide her nationality. At first, she thought of replying in Korean, but she dismissed the idea. She only knew some phrases and was not sure she could feign speaking Korean for any significant amount of time. Instead, she made the impulsive, desperate decision to remain silent no matter what.

As they disembarked the boat, she reluctantly followed the other women as they marched in line towards the village. A deep unease settled in the pit of Sarah's stomach; the air was charged with tension. The boatmen's strategic positioning—one at the front and one at the back of the line—felt deliberate. Were they making sure no one attempted to escape? Sarah's mind raced, considering every possibility. The clumsy flip-flops clinging to her feet removed any notion of running away. Even if she managed to fling them off, the soft beach sand would slow her down. She felt trapped, caught in a web she didn't fully understand, hoping for an opportunity, any opportunity, to present itself.

As they approached a semi-abandoned fishing village, Sarah's eyes were drawn to a picturesque Thai cottage nestled amid a grove of mango trees. Their ripe, golden fruit dangled temptingly from the branches, casting elongated shadows on the ground. Surrounding the cottage was a joyous array of tropical flora that seemed to burst with color. Bright pink bougainvillea with thick ancient vines supported by thin wooden trellises and wild frangipanis added their sweet fragrance to the air. Their white and pink petals contrasted starkly with their rich green foliage.

The pathetic irony was not lost on Sarah, who loved teaching literary devices to her freshmen students. She swallowed hard and felt tears form in her eyes at the thought that she might never step foot in her classroom again. Yes, it was a sterile, modern room, and not all her students loved literature, but it was her safe haven. Teaching gave her comfort and routine. Helping young people become adults provided a purpose. *Was it all over so soon?* Sarah felt her heart sink. She wiped her eyes and kept on walking. She was not going to show her captors how much she was hurting. But the feeling of being a lamb led to slaughter did not escape her.

As they stepped onto the compacted gravel track that led to the nearest cottage, an idea began to form in Sarah's mind. Seeing the village ahead, she made a split-second decision. Without a moment's hesitation, Sarah kicked off her footwear and broke into a run, heading straight for the village center. For a fleeting moment, Sarah felt free. But her feet were not used to running barefoot. Every step hurt, and she was not as fast as she imagined she would be.

Her only hope was that the suddenness of her escape would inspire the other two women to do the same. If they all ran in different directions, it would distract the men and give at least one of them a chance to get away and alert the authorities. But to her horror, they chose the same direction as her. Their strides were swift and determined, closing the distance between her and them rapidly.

Sarah's heart pounded in her chest as she heard them close behind her. The men shouted at each other in Thai, determined not to let Sarah escape. Just as she was about to turn a corner, a hand gripped her arm, pulling her to a stop. Breathless and panicked, Sarah turned to see one of the Thai women, her face mixed with anger and relief. The other woman caught up with them and grabbed Sarah's other arm.

It was then that the truth dawned on her. These women weren't fellow captives; they were accomplices in whatever scheme the boatmen were part of. This realization sent a chill down her spine, and her mind spun with questions. When they were all sitting quietly on the boat, the women must have thought she was with the boatmen, and the boatmen must have assumed she was with the two women. Her sudden escape, however, made it clear to both groups that she didn't belong.

CHAPTER 12

THE CLIMB

The morning air was fresh and invigorating at the start of the hike to Khao Ra. Tall, slender bamboo shoots lined the narrow dirt pathway, their leaves rustling in the early breeze. Vibrant wildflowers, including orchids in outrageously beautiful hues of pink and purple, dotted the edges of the trail.

Harry pulled up at the trailhead on her moped, the noise of the engine fracturing the scene's tranquility. As she quickly killed the engine, she noticed Pierre, Dominique, and Connor already waiting. Pierre adjusted the straps on his light daypack while Dominique chatted with Connor.

"*Bonjour*, Harry!" Pierre greeted her warmly, his eyes lighting up. "We invited Connor too; I hope is okay for you."

"Yes, of course. Morning guys," Harry responded with a nod, swinging her leg off the moped.

Dominique smiled, her eyes scanning Harry. "You look a little tired. Did you get some rest after yesterday's events?"

"Hardly," Harry confessed. "I was busy all night going over what might have happened and worrying about Sarah, but I can use the distraction. Maybe if I clear my head, I will be able to think better. You know how sometimes, when you get stuck on a problem, you can't solve it until you do something else? I hope that will be the case today."

"I know what you mean," Connor added. "It happens to me all the time. The best thing is to get out. I also needed some space after everything that's happened."

"And have you heard from Euclid? Is he okay?" Dominique asked.

"He went with Somchai to the police station to give a formal statement and provide some more personal details about Sarah," Harry explained. "He's quite worried. He thinks the detective suspects him of foul play, but I'm not sure. I think the police are just doing their job. They usually interview the partners and close family first."

"That's true," Dominique agreed. "But I can't imagine Euclid having anything to do with Sarah's disappearance. Personally, I fear there was a terrible accident. Maybe she went out on a boat that night and drowned... Perhaps a boat has gone missing. Did they check?"

The thought of her friend drowning at sea made Harry quite upset. Feeling the need to change the topic, Pierre began explaining the day's route, saying, "Alright, let's leave it at the back of us for now, *mes amis*... So, we will follow this trail until we reach an open space. From there, we go up and up, but the view from the top is *magnifique*. We should be there by noon."

Harry listened intently, appreciating Pierre's natural leadership. "How difficult is the hike?"

"For an old couple like us? It's manageable. Just watch out for slippery patches, especially after yesterday's rain," Dominique said encouragingly.

Pierre nodded. "Yes, and drink a lot of water."

The group chatted a bit longer, excited about the adventure ahead. After a few more minutes of preparation and light banter, they began their journey towards the peak of Khao Ra.

Walking side by side, Harry and Pierre trod lightly up the path. She noticed that Pierre seemed very agile and accustomed to tackling such trails.

"Is hiking an activity you do often?" Harry inquired.

Pierre responded with a bright smile, "*Oui*, we love it. Everywhere we go for holiday, we find places to walk. The mountains, the forests, it is… *comment dit-on*? Rejuvenating."

Walking closely behind them with Connor, Dominique joined in, "It's true. We love nature. We always try to take our vacations close to forests and mountains. Walking makes you forget about your problems."

Harry agreed, feeling the calming effects of the surroundings on her own troubled mind. The raucous calls of exotic birds could be heard from the dense tree canopy above, mingling with the sounds of a nearby babbling brook somewhere in the undergrowth. Butterflies in brilliant shades of metallic blue and orange flitted between the flowers while the occasional cheeky squirrel darted up a tree trunk, ready to play hide-and-seek with the intrepid hikers.

"You both seem so full of energy. How do you find time to exercise and keep fit? I've been told by my doctor to exercise every day. I'm supposed to stretch and do yoga, but life gets in the way. I try to find time, but it's not always easy."

Dominique listened compassionately. "I know what you mean. It's not easy, even for us, to find time to go for a hike or to meditate. That's why we've decided to retire this year."

Harry was surprised to hear that. Dominique and Pierre both seemed to be in their mid-fifties, still far from the normal age of retirement. She asked them about it.

"That's true. We are in our fifties, but we don't want to wait until we're too old to enjoy life. I'm thinking of starting a small business. Yoga, wellness... things to help the mind and body."

Pierre beamed with pride. "*Mon chérie* has many talents. She's ... *incroyable.*"

Walking with a youthful spring in his step, Connor seemed impressed with the couple's plan. "That sounds great! I agree with you. There's no point in waiting until you're too old to do the things you love. You know, my own parents have been talking about moving to Spain for decades. They were sick and tired of the Irish weather. But then my dad was diagnosed with MS in his late fifties, and it wasn't really possible anymore for them to move to another country and start from scratch. You know, the language barrier and the doctors. They still regret not moving to Spain when they were younger." He paused for a moment, reflecting. "In fact, I've been thinking about some changes myself. Career-wise, you know? Life's too short to be stuck doing something you don't love."

"Ah, *c'est vrai,*" Dominique responded. "It's important to follow your heart."

The group continued their ascent, sharing more about their dreams and aspirations, with the Thai nature as a beautiful backdrop to their light conversation.

Harry took a sip of water from her bottle and glanced over at Dominique and Pierre. "It's so interesting to hear about the lifepaths people take. Before I ventured into travel blogging, I had a steady job at a lifestyle magazine in New York. But somehow, it wasn't enough. I was not happy living in my tiny studio apartment. As a writer, I spent many hours a day trapped inside that box. Also, my job wasn't really fulfilling. I used to interview New York celebrities in their opulent homes. You know the magazine feature where you have stunning photos of a celebrity posing next to a set of very expensive pots in a stylish kitchen, implying that she's going to cook for friends or pretending to read a book while reclining on the biggest, whitest sofa you've ever seen?"

Dominique and Connor chuckled a little at Harry's sarcastic remarks about the rich and famous she used to work with.

"It was all so staged and so fake. I was disappointed with myself," Harry concluded. "I didn't feel proud of my work, and I definitely didn't enjoy it. But it's all in the past now. So, what did you two do before you decided to retire?"

"I was a social worker. I helped immigrant families adjust to their new life in France. It was a vocation for me—very fulfilling but not always rewarding, and definitely stressful. Humans don't enjoy accepting a stranger's advice or opinion on their lives, and they don't always see what's best for them. Plus, they often bring their cultural heritage and past experiences that can hold them back from doing well in the new situation. So, while I have some success stories, I also have many disappointments. But that's common in any social work, I think," Dominique said, her gaze distant. "The last few years have been affecting my health badly more and more. I discovered that I had been *grincer*, ... you, know, grinding my teeth unconsciously, and my hair started to fall out. It's all stress-related. So, it was time to go."

"And what about Pierre?" Harry asked.

He puffed out his chest in mock pride. "I was a *pompier*—how do you say? A firefighter. Many years running into burning buildings," he said, laughing. "It's perhaps why I appreciate the calm of nature so much now."

"That's incredible!" Harry exclaimed. "Both of you had such commendable jobs."

Dominique added, "Yes, maybe, but even we had our small cottage in Normandy and rewarding careers, something was missing. A certain... *je ne sais quoi*."

Connor, who had been listening intently, joined in. "Your life sounds dreamy to me. A quiet cottage, rewarding jobs... To be honest, I'd love to swap places with you. Working for different banks these past five years has been an absolute nightmare. The politics, the stress of deadlines, the long hours."

"Ah, *c'est la vie*, my friend. Sometimes, what looks perfect outside, it is not so inside. Each person has their own journey, you see," Pierre mused. "For me, your life is perfect. You are young and... *santé*, and you have money to travel. This *travail nomade*, the nomadic work, it did not exist when we were young."

"That's true," Dominique agreed. "There are more interesting jobs nowadays for young people. I'm so glad to see you two taking advantage of your opportunities."

The little group of acquaintances moved forward, each lost in their thoughts, soberly reflecting on their choices and life paths as they ascended the tropical mountain.

Harry tilted her head coyly towards Connor, a friendly smile playing on her lips. "I've heard some interesting stories about your transition from hacker to bank security expert. Rumor has it you did a little unauthorized digital exploring in your youth. Is that true?"

Connor laughed, his face reddening. "Ah, so word's got around, has it? Alright, alright, you've caught me, the man is 'guilty as charged'. When I was seventeen, I somehow found my way into the postal system's intranet."

"And what was your grand plan?" Harry teased. "Get some free stamps?"

Grinning sheepishly, Connor replied, "I changed the default message for undeliverable emails to say 'Return to Sender, Address Unknown, No Such Number, No Such Zone', you know, like the Elvis song? I thought it was a harmless joke."

Harry laughed. "That's brilliant, yet so... silly."

Connor continued, "Ah, well, not everyone saw it that way. But, lucky for me, the prosecutor figured I was just a daft eejit, not meaning any real harm. So, instead of jail, I got slapped with community service, checking the local town hall's internet security for holes—free of charge, mind you. Turns out, I had a bit of a gift for finding weak spots and patching them up. And that's how I fell into cybersecurity. The rest, as they say, is history."

The group continued their merry way up the trail, surrounded by incredible natural beauty. The thick jungle on either side of the path created a tunnel of green, with bright sunlight occasionally breaking through the canopy, giving the ground before them a luminescent texture. They passed close by a small mountain stream, clear and inviting. The shallow water, just a meter across, danced over the pebbles, making a pleasant gurgling sound that accompanied their rhythmic footsteps. Later, they reached a majestic reservoir higher up on the side of the mountain, a calm body of precious water perfectly reflecting the vivid blues of the sky and the verdant greens of the surrounding foliage.

As the party journeyed on, Pierre chuckled. "You know, that little stream back there, it reminds me of when Dominique and I, we were lost in the Yosemite National Park."

Dominique rolled her eyes playfully. "Oh, *mon Dieu*! Don't remind me! It was during our honeymoon trip to California."

Harry and Connor exchanged amused glances, prompting Pierre to share the tale. "Well, what happened was that we got lost *absolument*. I thought we were taking an easy route, you know? But halfway, I realize the map I was using—it was upside down! By the time I see my mistake, we are on *a comment dit-on ? Un rebord ?*" Pierre mimed the word for 'ledge'. "It was impossible to continue."

"And to make it worse, my shoe—it got stuck in a, uh, crevice," Dominique cut in, "and when I try to pull it free, *pouf!*—it fell apart!"

Harry and Connor listened with awe and disbelief as Pierre continued, "So there we are, tired and hungry, with Dominique in one shoe and the night coming fast. We had to walk back *tout le chemin!* At first, I think maybe we sleep in the mountains until the sun comes up. But then we hear the American coyotes howling, and we decide, no, no—we go on. I could not sleep anyway."

"I was a bit scared myself—not so much of the coyotes, but the, how you say, *oirs noirs*," Pierre added. "*Heureusement*, we have no food to attract the animals. When we finally arrive at our place, it is very dark, and our host, he is wondering if he should call for a rescue!"

"Back then, mobile phones were still a *nouveauté*, and only rich people had them," Dominique said, explaining to the young people the reason why they hadn't called for help.

Connor grinned, eager to share his own misadventure. "Ah, sounds like quite the adventure! Reminds me of the time I thought it'd be grand to climb Croagh Patrick with me cousin Seamus. Sure, it's popular with tourists and pilgrims, but our trip? Far from ordinary, I tell ya.

"We're halfway up the mountain when Seamus, swearing he's got the gift to 'talk to leprechauns', decides to wander off the trail looking for 'golden clovers'. Next thing I know, we're lost—stuck knee-deep in a bog. And as if that wasn't enough, I got tired and plonked meself right on top of an ant nest!"

Everyone laughed as Connor went on, "So there we are, covered head-to-toe in mud and ant bites, trying to find our way back as the sun's going down. Just as we're starting to panic, we stumble upon a group of Benedictine monks on a silent walking retreat. They can't say a word to us, but they still manage to guide us back to the main path with hand signals and a few stern looks."

Dominique chuckled. "And I thought our story was dramatic!"

"Believe me," Connor laughed, "after that, I stick to well-marked trails and leave the leprechauns to their own business!"

The group continued their happy hike up the mountain while sharing slightly exaggerated stories of their vacation misadventures.

Reaching the summit of Khao Ra, the group was greeted with a panorama that took their breath away. The lush expanse of tropical forest was spread out before them, an undulating sea of green that stretched as far as the eye could see. The vivid emerald canopy was broken here and there by the silver gleam of a distant stream or the deeper green of a hidden lake.

From another perspective, the distant coastline of Koh Phangan was visible, a delicate thread of golden sand that met the shimmering turquoise waters of the Gulf of Thailand. The play of light on the water gave it sparkling magic, and far-off islands dotted the horizon, fading into misty silhouettes. The gently sloping side of the mountain also showcased an intricate pattern of terraced rice paddies, their dark, watery surfaces gleaming under the sun.

Above, the sky was an endless stretch of blue, with a few fluffy white clouds drifting lazily by. Majestic birds of prey soared on the thermals, their cries echoing faintly.

Another small group of tourists was already at the summit, their chatter and laughter blending with the sounds of nature. They were scattered around, some taking photos, some simply sitting on the ground and soaking in the beauty, while others consulted maps and discussed their descent.

The gentle breeze at that elevation was refreshing, carrying with it the sweet scent of blooming flowers from the valleys below and the subtle saltiness of the sea. It was a place of tranquility and awe, a reminder of Nature's majesty and the smallness of human endeavors in the grand scheme of things.

As Dominique and Pierre wandered around the clearing, taking selfies and chatting with the other hikers, Harry took a moment to reflect on the events that had taken place at the Hideaway. Was Sarah's disappearance related to Zoë's death? Had Sarah witnessed something she shouldn't have? Had she unwittingly discovered the identity of the con artist Zoë was investigating?

"If I can find Zoë's killer, it might lead me to Sarah," she murmured aloud.

Behind her, Connor's voice broke into her reverie. "What do you mean *Zoë's killer*? I thought she drowned. That's what everyone's been saying."

Harry turned sharply, her face flushing. She hadn't meant for anyone to hear her words, let alone Connor. But as she met his gaze, something told her she could trust him.

Harry motioned for him to step aside with her. "Look," she began in a low voice, "I don't think Zoë's death was accidental. She told me she was working on a story for a magazine in New York. She was about to expose someone... someone big, as a conman or a scammer. I think that might have something to do with her death."

Connor's eyes widened in surprise and concern. "That's a dangerous game to play. If what you're saying is true, you might be in danger too, especially if it comes out that you knew what Zoë was doing and suspect foul play."

Harry glanced up at Connor with a hint of desperation in her eyes. "We need to get Zoë's laptop. It must be still in her hut. The police didn't seem to take anything from there."

"How do you know that?"

"I looked through the porch window when no one was around. Her things were scattered around. Since the police assume she drowned, I don't think they are going through her private affairs. I'm sure her laptop must be there. No journalist travels without one."

Connor raised an eyebrow. "But the hut has been sealed off by the police, has it not?"

Harry gave him a cheeky look that clearly communicated she had every intention of bypassing that minor obstacle. She needed to see if there was any evidence on the laptop.

"From hacking into postal systems to breaking and entering in Thailand. My life certainly has taken on an adventurous turn, hasn't it? Just promise we won't end up in a Thai jail, alright?"

Harry chuckled, appreciating the light-heartedness he brought to the situation. "Deal," she replied with a smile. "But I wouldn't worry. If the police had wanted the laptop, they'd have taken it. Think about it as helping them along the way, nudging them toward the truth."

Connor was not convinced by Harry's excuse but agreed to help her.

CHAPTER 13

IN THE SHADOWS OF THE NIGHT

The darkness surrounding Mango Moon Hideaway was profound, interrupted only by the occasional shimmering glint of moonlight reflecting off the glossy obsidian leaves of some nearby trees. The familiar distant hum of conversations and music that usually wafted through the night at the resort was conspicuously absent, giving the place an eerie, abandoned feel.

Harry crouched low behind the bamboo wall of Zoë's hut, checking her watch for the umpteenth time. It was a couple of minutes past 3 a.m. Where was Connor? The silence blanketing the resort was unnerving, amplifying every incidental leaf rustle and insect chirp to startling levels. She wondered if this was how it felt every night at the resort when the cheerful ambiance she was used to was replaced by a secret, silent darkness.

She heard a faint rustling in the distance that grew gradually louder until she could discern soft footsteps. Connor emerged from the shadows, looking a bit flustered.

"You're late," Harry whispered, a hint of annoyance in her voice.

Connor raised an apologetic hand. "Sorry, had to make sure no one saw me."

She nodded, taking a deep breath. "Okay, here's the plan: the bathroom window has a simple latch lock. We can get it open using a piece of folded paper."

Connor looked at her quizzically. "You sure about this?"

Harry smirked. "Trust me. Slide the paper underneath the lock, between the window frame and the window. Then, gently move it up, and the hook should slip off. I tried it on the one in my hut. It works."

Connor seemed impressed. "Alright, let's do it. I'll keep a lookout. Just be quick, yeah?"

She nodded, feeling a rush of adrenaline. As she moved stealthily towards the window, Harry thought about how far she had come, from a travel blogger to a night stalker breaking and entering. She shook off the thought of the possible punishment she risked and focused on the task at hand. If Zoë's death wasn't accidental, she wouldn't be able to look herself in the mirror. Time was of the essence, and she couldn't afford to make any mistakes.

In the dense silence, the rubberized squeak of Harry's dishwashing gloves seemed almost deafening. Connor glanced skeptically at them, clearly wondering why on earth she was wearing them.

Seeing his confusion, Harry whispered, "I couldn't find any latex gloves. Didn't want to leave fingerprints. You never know how thorough the police might get if they decide to investigate further."

Connor nodded in understanding, his eyes reflecting a mix of amusement and appreciation for her improvisation. He swiftly took off his cotton beanie, stretching it out towards her. "Here," he whispered. "Put this on."

Harry was about to question how useful the beanie might be when it dawned on her—the shock of pink in her hair would be a dead giveaway. "Smart thinking," she whispered back, carefully tucking away every strand of her hair under the head cover.

Once she was suitably 'kitted up', Harry turned her attention back to the window. With a steadying breath, she slid a piece of folded paper into the tiny space between the latch and the frame, gently nudging the hook upward. There was a soft, satisfying click as the latch released.

She paused for a second, looking back at Connor. They exchanged a brief nod, steeling themselves for what lay inside.

The dim light from Harry's cell phone pierced the darkness of Zoë's hut, casting long, wavering shadows over its interior. The sight was oddly haunting: a room frozen in time, with clothes and personal items strewn about, just as their owner had left them. Harry's heart pounded so loudly in her chest that she half-expected Connor to comment on it.

She took a deep breath to steady herself and looked around methodically. Her light first caught the gleam of a half-empty bottle of red wine next to a single glass. The sight sent a shiver down her spine. The mundane act of enjoying a drink before a party was creepily juxtaposed with the chilling mystery that had unfolded later that fatal night.

Next to the bottle lay a makeup bag, its contents spilled out onto the table's surface. Harry briefly shined her light on the table, noting the mascara, lipstick, and a compact mirror before moving on. This wasn't what she was looking for.

Harry's gaze fell on the bed. She crouched down, pulling out a suitcase from beneath it. With a faint hope in her heart, she unzipped the suitcase, only to find more clothes, toiletries, and a few personal items, but no laptop or tablet.

Her desperation grew. She felt like she was missing something crucial. "Surely Zoë would've had something to take notes on," she muttered to herself, her voice low and shaky in the room's silence. An investigative reporter on an undercover assignment wouldn't go completely analog.

With increasing frustration, she checked the nightstand, the shelves, and even the small reading nook in the corner of the hut. Still nothing.

Connor, keeping watch by the window, whispered, "Any luck?"

Harry let out a defeated sigh. "Nothing. I can't find any of her tech, which doesn't make any sense. She was a social media influencer. She must have used a tablet or a laptop to manipulate her photos and write posts. No one can do it professionally on the phone. You'd go mad working like that."

The unsettling idea that someone might have gotten to the laptop before them loomed in the back of her mind.

Harry, feeling an overwhelming sense of disappointment, turned off her phone's light, and the hut was again enveloped in pitch darkness. Every lead, every hint, every shred of hope she had seemed to dissipate into the thick, humid air of the unventilated room.

Emerging from the hut, she gently closed the window and gave it a firm tug, ensuring it latched properly. The night around them was quiet, save for the distant chorus of crickets and frogs. Harry pulled off the cotton beanie, allowing her pink hair to tumble free, and removed her rubber gloves, making sure they didn't snap. She looked at Connor with a mixture of exasperation and determination.

"Find anything?" Connor asked, his voice breaking the silence.

Shaking her head, Harry whispered back, "There's nothing. Not even a single scrap of paper to suggest she was here on a job. It's like she wasn't even a reporter."

Connor frowned. "That doesn't make sense. You think someone got there before us?"

"I'm not sure," Harry responded thoughtfully. "But if Zoë had any electronic devices, they are gone. There's a power bank charging in one of the wall sockets. She must have used it as a back-up to run her laptop while she traveled."

Connor nodded slowly, processing the implications. "So, how do we find the laptop?"

Harry sighed, gazing up at the vast starry sky, seeking inspiration. "If she was indeed murdered, whoever killed her must have taken the laptop to destroy any evidence she had gathered."

Suddenly, Harry signaled for Connor to be quiet, and they both ducked behind the thick trunk of a nearby banana tree. A male voice, hushed and seemingly engaged in a secretive conversation, was approaching them. The sound was so faint that, at first, Harry couldn't make out who it might belong to.

Drawing closer, the voice became clearer, and snippets of German reached their ears. "*Ja, natürlich bin ich mir dessen bewusst,*" the voice asserted. There was a pause, the rustling of leaves and footsteps the only discernible sounds. And then: "*Aber ich denke, das Problem ist gelöst. Du solltest dir darüber keine Sorgen mehr machen.*"

As the words drifted off, fading into the distance, Harry and Connor peeked out from their hiding spot, exchanging bewildered looks.

Connor broke the silence, whispering, "Was that Reggie?"

Harry nodded in response, her brows furrowing in deep thought. "It definitely sounded like him. But who on earth was he talking to? And why would he be on the phone speaking German at this ungodly hour?"

Chapter 14

THE CAVE

The breakfast room at the Hideaway was bathed in the warm, golden hues of the morning sun. Light streamed in through the room's large windows, casting delicate patterns on the walls and tables. Palm leaves outside swayed gently, their silhouettes engaged in a playful shadow dance on the room's polished floor.

Long wooden tables were laden with an assortment of breakfast options. The generous spread included an array of tropical fruits, including mango, papaya, and rambutan, alongside bowls of creamy yogurt and granola. A hot food station sizzled with traditional favorites: eggs made to order—scrambled, poached, or sunny side up—and crisp bacon slices. A basket overflowed with freshly baked pastries, from plain croissants to *pain au chocolat*. For those looking for local delicacies, there were dishes consisting of fried rice with vegetables and spicy noodles. The beverages offered ranged from fresh fruit juices to steaming pots of coffee and tea.

The atmosphere in the breakfast room was surprisingly lively, with the soft buzz of relaxed conversation filling the air. Guests chatted, planning their day or sharing stories from the previous evening. A soothing playlist of world music added to the serene ambiance, interspersed occasionally with the distant sounds of tropical birdsong.

To Harry, however, this idyllic setting felt disturbingly out of place. Glancing around, she found it hard to stomach the ease with which the other guests seemed to have moved on from the recent tragedy. Here they were, laughing, planning trips, and enjoying their breakfast while one young woman was dead and another had disappeared into thin air.

She tore a piece off her buttery croissant, but her appetite was overshadowed by her feelings of dismay. Harry's attention was attracted the expat newspaper lying next to her cup of black coffee. The front page bore a large photo of Zoë, looking radiant and full of life. The headline below read 'FOAM-TASTROPHY'. The distasteful pun was the last straw. Harry often thought of puns as the lowest form of humor, and to use one when reporting on a death seemed to be the lowest form of journalism. The insensitivity of the headline, combined with the general apathy around her in the breakfast room, intensified her resolve to find the truth.

Snapping out of her reverie, Harry looked up to see Somchai's warm and reassuring face. The shining silver pot she held up in offering mirrored the comforting light in her kind eyes. "Would you like some more coffee, Harry?" she inquired kindly, the familiar and gentle cadence of her voice offering a momentary reprieve from Harry's consuming thoughts.

Harry managed a meek, appreciative smile. "Yes, please, Somchai. I could use all the caffeine I can get." As the aromatic coffee streamed into her cup, Harry's mind raced with thoughts of the previous night. The looming questions, the shadows, the voice in the dark... But of course, she couldn't share last night's events with Somchai.

Instead, seeking information, she asked, "Has there been any official statement from the police about Zoë?" She hoped Somchai might be able to offer some new insight, maybe something she had missed.

Somchai paused for a long moment, placing the coffee pot carefully back on the table. "Yes, the police made an announcement on our local TV channel this morning." She gestured towards the newspaper on Harry's table. "It's all in there too. They believe Zoë's death was an unfortunate accident—a so-called 'secondary drowning'. They've found no evidence suggesting foul play; there was alcohol in her blood, of course, but no drugs. Zoë was young and healthy, so they ruled out organ failure or natural causes."

Harry's heart sank. "Really?" She had hoped that the post-mortem would reveal the truth about Zoë's death. Perhaps she had been given some drugs that caused her to suffocate... But the police seemed to be fixed on their theory of secondary drowning. The facts thus far all felt overwhelming.

"Why? What's wrong, Harry? Don't you think it was an accident?"

Harry sincerely appreciated Somchai's kindness. She didn't want to lie to her. "To be honest, I'm not 100% convinced Zoë drowned, but then I'm not a detective," she whispered.

Somchai assented, giving Harry a comforting pat on the shoulder. "Stay strong, Harry. Things will become clearer with time."

"By the way, Somchai, I wanted to ask you about one of the guests who was here when we arrived. His name was Forrest or something like that. He had long blond hair that he pulled back into a ponytail. A surfer, I think."

"I know who you mean. Grove, not Forrest. He checked out yesterday. He said he was too traumatized to stay. Apparently, the police interviewed him for a long time. He was the last one seen dancing with Zoë."

"Did he say where he was going?"

"No, no idea."

With that, Somchai moved on to attend to the other guests, leaving Harry to grapple with her thoughts once more. Could Grove be the fraudster that Zoë was talking about? Is that why she had befriended him? Harry had seen her talking to him on several occasions. She had to find him and speak to him.

Encouraged by this new line of inquiry, Harry reached across the table and opened the expat newspaper, bracing herself for what she was about to read.

FOAM-TASTROPHY:

Backpacking Influencer Dies after Scuba Diving

By C. Huxley, *Expat Daily*

KOH PHANGAN – Tragedy struck Mango Moon Hideaway two nights ago as Zoë Kessler, a 28-year-old travel blogger from New York City, was found unresponsive after a popular foam party at the resort. The young influencer, known for her exuberant posts capturing the essence of far-flung destinations, was reportedly enjoying a few cocktails with friends when the unfortunate incident occurred.

Ms. Kessler, a seasoned traveler who had made a name for herself in the digital world, had spent the day exploring the island's crystal-clear waters on a scuba diving expedition. According to local authorities, it appears her death was caused by secondary drowning—a rare but serious condition where water inhaled during swimming or diving triggers a fatal reaction in the lungs, sometimes hours after leaving the water.

A statement from the police detailed that Ms. Kessler's scuba diving activities earlier in the day in question likely contributed to her sudden and tragic death. "Secondary drowning can be difficult to detect and often presents symptoms such as difficulty breathing, coughing, and fatigue," explained Detective Niran, who is leading the investigation. "It's crucial for anyone who has inhaled water, even in small amounts, to seek medical attention immediately."

Guests at the Hideaway recalled seeing Zoë throughout the day, capturing the island's picturesque scenery with her camera. "She had a passion for documenting her experiences," noted one guest who preferred to remain unnamed. "Her cell phone camera was never far from her side, whether she was photographing a sunset or enjoying a meal."

Zoë Kessler's untimely death serves as a somber reminder of the potential dangers that can accompany the relentless pursuit of adventure, even in paradise. While her vibrant posts inspired many to chase their own dreams, her sudden passing highlights the importance of understanding and respecting the risks that come with engaging in certain activities.

As her social media accounts are now inundated with messages of condolence, one can't help but reflect on the delicate balance between living in the moment and being driven to share those moments with the rest of the world.

Harry's hands trembled as she put the newspaper down. The audacity of the journalist to paint Zoë as a frivolous, directionless hipster irked her beyond words. True, Zoë had her flaws, but she was more than a bundle of millennial clichés. She had depth, ambition, and a real story to tell—one that had now been overshadowed by this superficial and somewhat judgmental portrayal of her work. Righteous anger welled up inside her, and Harry made a silent vow to herself: She would set the record straight and discover the truth about the person Zoë was investigating.

Harry's somber thoughts were disrupted by a French-accented voice. "You seem quite perturbed, *mademoiselle.*"

Startled, Harry looked up to find Pierre. His deep-set blue eyes bore a hint of concern.

Harry let out a sigh, pointing at the newspaper. "This article. It's... it's so distasteful."

Pierre stepped closer to Harry to look at the newspaper, squinting at the small-type. "Ah, I haven't read this. I only read French news on my phone. What does it say?"

Harry summarized for him, emphasizing how they depicted Zoë as some vapid millennial wanderer. "It's so unfair to her memory," she concluded, frustration evident in her voice.

Pierre nodded, sympathizing with her sentiment. "That's true. She wasn't just interested in seeking experiences for her Instagram. She was a nature-loving person."

Harry blinked in surprise. "Nature-loving?" She raised an eyebrow. To her knowledge, Zoë wasn't one for gardening or animals. "I mean, I've never seen her with a pet or even a houseplant."

Pierre chuckled softly. "Ah, perhaps I did not use the right term. What I mean is she seemed to be in tune with the world around her. Not plants, specifically, but the energy. On several occasions, I saw her hiking in the evening outside the Hideaway and exploring the jungle. Once, I found her meditating very early in the morning. She said she was drawing energy from the rising sun."

Harry was taken aback. This was an aspect of Zoë she hadn't been privy to. "Drawing energy from the sun? That... doesn't sound at all like the Zoë I knew."

Pierre shrugged, a philosophical smile gracing his lips. "People have many layers, no? Perhaps there was more to Zoë than even she revealed."

Nodding, Harry felt renewed adamance.

"Is everything OK?" Pierre asked, noting the change in Harry's demeanor.

"It's just surprising to hear about this side of Zoë. I've never known her to be keen on nature or meditation."

Pierre shrugged slightly. "She seemed very peaceful when I saw her up there."

An idea began to take shape in Harry's mind, but she kept it to herself. "Would you show me where she used to go to meditate? I'm curious to see the place."

Pierre took a sip of his coffee, looking thoughtful. "Of course, I can take you there after I finish this coffee. But it's a bit secluded."

"That's alright," Harry responded, trying to keep her eagerness in check. "It might give me a better understanding of Zoë."

Harry's mind was already racing ahead.

"Is there any news about Sarah?" Pierre asked while finishing his coffee.

"Unfortunately, no. I'm worried sick, and I can't imagine how Euclid feels. He's been in and out of the police station giving statements, but there are no leads. The police made a public appeal on TV today, hoping that witnesses would come forward. Someone at the party must have seen where Sarah went."

"That's a good idea. I hope they find her soon." Pierre set the cup on the table. "Let's go, Harry. Ready to explore a little?"

"Right behind you."

As they began their walk through the Hideaway resort, the familiar sounds of laughter and chatter enveloped them.

Approaching the pool area, Harry couldn't help but notice how quickly things had returned to normal. The yellow police tape that had cordoned off the scene of Zoë's tragic end was now gone. Instead, guests occupied the sun-loungers, some sipping on fruity cocktails, others engrossed in their books. The soft murmur of conversation blended with the gentle lapping of the pool water.

Shaking off the surreal juxtaposition of past and present, Harry followed Pierre. They soon left the manicured beauty of the resort behind and veered left into the thick underbrush of the jungle. Only the sound of birds and distant drone of flying insects accompanied them.

After walking a few meters, Pierre suddenly stopped and gently pushed aside some hanging vines, revealing a narrow, barely visible path. The trail was a mere subtle indentation in the earth, framed by ferns and overshadowed by tall trees. One would easily miss it unless one knew of its existence.

"This is it," Pierre announced.

Harry followed Pierre deeper into the jungle.

The path wound its way upwards, becoming steeper with every step. The dense canopy above shielded them from the sun, but occasional beams of light managed to pierce through, casting stippled patterns on the ground. With each stride, the air grew cooler, in contrast to the tropical warmth of the resort below. The earth beneath their feet was soft and damp from the frequent afternoon monsoon rains.

The sounds of the jungle again enveloped them in a melodic symphony of exuberant life. Distant bird calls echoed, their notes sharp and clear, while the rustle of leaves hinted at unseen creatures scurrying in the underbrush, going about their hidden business. Every so often, the trill of a cicada or the croak of a frog rose above the ambient noise.

As they continued their ascent, Harry's curiosity grew. "Pierre," she began, her voice slightly breathless from the climb, "how did you discover this path? It's so hidden."

Pierre chuckled softly. "I... how to say... *j'adore*... I love finding places that are hidden. Tourist routes, they have many people. I think the real beauty, it's... in secret spots and hidden paths. One morning, very early, before the resort wakes up, I come here. Sun just starting to... *comment dit-on*... rise? And there," he said, pointing to a serene-looking clearing ahead, "I see Zoë."

He paused as they approached a gentle curve in the path. "Just over there, I saw her." He motioned to a small clearing bathed in a soft glow.

Harry looked at the spot, trying to visualize the scene. "And she was... meditating?"

Pierre nodded. "*Oui*, yes. She seemed so... in harmony? I didn't want to disturb, but curiosity, it got better of me. I approach and ask, 'Why are you here so early?' She speaks of... mindfulness. She says this place, it's good for her to... contemplate, to think."

They both stood there for a moment, taking in the beauty of the clearing. The gentle sounds of the jungle, the whisper of the wind, and the soft play of light created a magical, angelic atmosphere. Pierre was right; it was easy to see why Zoë, or anyone for that matter, would be drawn to such a spot. While secluded and difficult to find, the spot itself wasn't too far from the Hideaway.

Harry looked intently at the peaceful clearing, but she wasn't entirely sold on the idea that Zoë frequented this area just for mindfulness practices. However, she refrained from voicing her doubts to Pierre.

She took a deep breath. "Thank you, Pierre. This means a lot to me. Would you mind if I spent some time alone here? Just to... reflect on Zoë's life."

"Of course," Pierre replied empathetically. "I... understand? It is very *tragique*. A young woman, full of life, gone just like that. It seems like an accident most cruel, no?"

Harry blinked back her emotions, choosing not to clarify her suspicions about Zoë's death to Pierre. "Thank you," she simply replied, her voice barely audible.

Pierre gave her a gentle smile. "*Prends ton temps*—take your time," he said. "I'll see you back at the Hideaway." With a soft rustle of leaves, Pierre disappeared back into the dense jungle.

Harry allowed herself a quiet moment, absorbing the atmosphere and piecing together the events leading up to Zoë's demise. The more she thought about it, the less sense it made. Once she felt Pierre was far enough away, she began to scour the area, looking for any abnormalities or signs that something might be hidden. And that's when she spotted it: a large flat rock standing almost vertical between a pair of ancient tree trunks. What made this rock peculiar was its lack of green moss—its clean gray surface stood out amidst the otherwise damp and overgrown jungle environment.

Approaching the rock, Harry's intuition told her that she might be onto something. The flat rock hid an opening between the trees, leading into a narrow passageway to a cave. The cave's interior was damp and cooler than the jungle outside, and the smell of earth enveloped Harry. She turned on her cell phone's torch and made her way further inside. The entrance was tight, forcing her to scrape her arms against the rough, rocky surface. But once she was through, the passageway expanded into a small cave.

The stillness was suddenly broken when a bat, disturbed by the intruder's light, flapped its wings in a frenzied panic, creating a gust of air and eerie shadows against the cave's walls. The bat's sudden appearance caused Harry to drop her phone, her heart racing. She squatted down and waited for a moment, catching her breath and listening to the fading sounds of the bat's wings as it flew deeper into the unknown recesses of the cave.

Once her initial shock passed, Harry quickly retrieved her phone and cautiously proceeded. Its torch revealed uneven ground, with jagged rocks protruding in some places and tree roots descending from the ceiling in others. But what caught her attention was a plastic box placed conspicuously against the wall.

Eagerly, she approached the container. The lid was sealed tight, but with a bit of effort, it clicked open. Inside, she found a laptop carefully encased in a sturdy plastic bag to protect it from the damp conditions of the cave.

Thoughts raced through her mind. Was this Zoë's secret hideaway? Why had she hidden her laptop here? And what could possibly be on it?

With the laptop secured in her grasp, Harry decided it was best to leave the cave and inspect its contents in the safety of her hut. She carefully retraced her steps, making her way out of the cave's mouth.

Chapter 15

EXPOSED

With its bamboo walls, simple palm leaf roof, and sparse wooden furnishings, the small Thai cottage Sarah found herself in would've been charming if it were not for her current predicament. Her wrists ached from the ropes that held her tightly. The dank humidity inside the hut made her brow sweat, and the sticky fabric of her clothes clung to her damp body, heightening her discomfort.

She'd been in the cottage for two nights now. One of the women had set up a rolled-up mattress on the floor for Sarah. During the day, the cottage was quiet as the boatmen and the women slept. Then, in the evening, they'd leave the cottage and disappear until the following day. Sarah struggled to understand the nature of the gang, but she was pretty sure that they thought she knew something, or why else would they keep her prisoner here? She was too scared to speak English and stuck to the idea of pretending to be mute. She wasn't sure if her captors were buying her act. Perhaps they were deciding what to do with her. She was sure her presence was a major inconvenience to them, but they would not let her go for some reason.

Sarah had spent many hours daydreaming and thinking of the events that had led to her current predicament over the past two days. She remembered the final hour of the foam party. It had been well past midnight when she tired of dancing. She had looked for Harry but couldn't find her. Then, she had seen Euclid and Connor deep in brotherly conversation at the bar. She had waved at them to say she was going to bed, but they hadn't noticed her. Walking towards her hut, she had felt a sudden urge to take a detour to the beach to take in the starry night. The stars and the moonlit sea had been magical. That's when she saw a boat beached on the sand. It had looked abandoned, so she decided to lie on a padded bench inside the boat and enjoy the stars. That was her last memory until she woke up at sea.

Across the room, the Thai women seemed at ease. They laughed and talked animatedly with the boatmen; short, stocky men with sun-worn faces and constant grins. The conversation flowed smoothly, a melody of a language she didn't understand, punctuated by shared laughter and casual gestures.

On a low table nearby, an elderly woman with wrinkles that mapped out a lifetime of experience was setting down some dishes. Her eyes were gentle, full of warmth and life, and her every move was deliberate and caring. Sarah was puzzled. How could such a tender-faced woman be a part of her kidnapping?

The table was adorned with a variety of dishes. There were bowls of green curry, succulent chunks of chicken, and a Thai eggplant dish. Beside this was a bowl of spicy papaya salad seasoned with fish sauce, chilies, and lime, with a handful of crushed peanuts sprinkled on top. There were also platters of sticky rice. The smell wafting from the table was a blend of spicy, tangy, and sweet aromas, making Sarah's stomach growl in response.

The third boatman seemed slightly out of place. He was taller, leaner, and with a more guarded expression than the other two. While he wasn't leading the conversation, the others felt his presence, especially when he reached over to put more rice onto his plate. It was evident that he held some position of power, even if he wasn't the ostensible leader of the group.

Trapped in her thoughts and the foreignness of her surroundings, Sarah felt a pang of hunger. The mouthwatering scent of the dishes served as a cruel reminder of her situation. Not only was she bound and held against her will, but she was also ravenous, yearning for a taste of the sumptuous food that was being eaten just meters away from her.

The atmosphere inside the Thai cottage was paradoxical. The simplicity and warmth of the scene—with its home-cooked food, easy conversations, and the gentle electric whisper of an overhead fan—was sharply contrasted by Sarah's grim reality. As she tried to reconcile the two, her situation became too much for her to bear, and she began to sob quietly.

Seeing Sarah's distress, the old woman uttered something sharply in Thai. The boatmen replied in a casual tone, but no one took any immediate action. That is, until the thin man stood up, clinking his eating utensils down onto the table. With a look of mild compassion, he prepared a plate for Sarah, piling it with rice, chicken, and a helping of green curry. He leaned down to untie her wrists, and for the first time in hours, Sarah felt the relief of unrestricted movement.

He took a bottle of water from the fridge and showed it to Sarah, who nodded gratefully. But as he went to fetch Sarah's plate of food, a sudden commotion erupted in the room. Sarah's heart raced as one of the women pointed at the television, urgently grabbing the remote to turn up the volume.

When Sarah followed the woman's gaze, she felt her stomach drop. There she was—her face on the large TV screen, hair slightly windblown, eyes filled with the joy from her last adventure. It was a selfie that she and Euclid had taken on their trip to the Grand Canyon. Euclid's face was cropped out of the shot on the TV screen, but she knew he was there, which made her sadder than she had ever felt before. *Will we ever be together again?* she thought to herself. The headline under the photo was in Thai and English: 'Missing American Tourist'. A Thai policeman was being interviewed by a reporter who, at the end of the news segment, translated everything into English, making an appeal for information to other tourists and local expats.

"While the police are emphasizing that there is no link between the recent tragedy at Mango Moon Hideaway and this unfortunate disappearance, one has to wonder if there could be a connection," the reporter finished in English as the camera panned out.

Another tragedy? Sarah's heart sank. *Has something happened to Euclid or Harry?*

But she did not have time to speculate as a wave of realization swept the room. Sarah's once unimportant presence had become the center of their focus. The undercurrent of tension was palpable. Every eye was now on her, analyzing, assessing. The old woman whispered something to the thin man, who looked at Sarah with an unreadable expression.

Sarah felt the atmosphere in the room shift from casual indifference to one of heightened alert. The anger behind those stares, combined with the news on the television, intensified her vulnerability. She felt like a cornered animal, surrounded and exposed, with nowhere to run.

CHAPTER 16

THE MESSAGE

Harry settled into the sofa in the corner of the hut, her eyes fixed on Connor, who was hunched over Zoë's laptop. The room was dimly lit, with only the amber hue of the setting sun filtering through the wooden blinds, casting elongated, horizontal shadows across the room. The rhythmic swoosh of the overhead cooling fan, paired with the staccato tapping of Connor's fingers, created a tense mood in the room.

"Any luck?" she inquired, watching him closely.

Connor sighed, pausing to stretch his back. "Not yet, but I have a few tricks up my sleeve."

Harry stood up from the sofa, intrigued. "Like what? Can't you just, I don't know, force your way in? I thought that's what hackers do. Just break into her laptop."

Connor smirked. "It's a little more nuanced than that. I could try brute forcing it, where I attempt every possible combination to crack the password. But it's time-consuming and loud—in a digital sense. It alerts the system. It's amateurish, in my opinion."

Harry gave Connor a questioning look. "So, what are the other methods?"

"Well," Connor began, "there are dictionary attacks. Instead of random combinations, I'd use a list of words or phrases commonly used as passwords, like 'password123' or 'iloveyou'."

Harry chuckled. "Sounds too easy."

"You'd be surprised," Connor continued. "Then there's phishing. But that requires tricking someone into giving up their credentials, usually by mimicking a trusted site or sending a fake email. That won't work in this case."

Harry thought for a moment. "What about those, uh, keyloggers? I read an article about them once."

"Yes, keyloggers record every keystroke. So, if I'd had access to Zoë's laptop earlier and installed one, I'd know her password by now. But that's not an option at the moment."

Harry sighed. "So, what're you going to do?"

"I'll try some common passwords first. If that doesn't work, I have a program that can potentially exploit vulnerabilities in the operating system to bypass the login screen."

Harry nodded, trusting Connor's expertise. "Alright, work your magic. We need whatever is on that laptop. In the meantime, I'll check her social media for clues of a possible password."

"Look for pet names and boyfriends," Connor suggested, cracking his knuckles. "Let's hope Zoë wasn't too tech-savvy." And with that, he dove back into his digital quest, his fingers flying across the keyboard.

Harry returned to the sofa. Comfortable once again, her eyes darted across her phone screen as she scrolled through Zoë's meticulously curated Instagram feed. Each post presented a seemingly carefree life characterized by picturesque sunsets, pristine beaches, and vibrant local cultures. Comments had poured in from followers and friends, complimenting the composition of the shots, the beauty of the locations, or simply expressing envy for the wanderlust-driven life Zoë portrayed.

"What an intricate façade!" Harry spoke to herself, her fingers pausing over a particularly candid shot of Zoë smiling against the backdrop of a cascading waterfall.

Connor glanced up. "What did you say?"

Harry shook her head, still engrossed in the digital mirage before her. "It's all too perfect, too orchestrated. Every post, every caption. It's like... like she's playing a part."

Connor frowned, tapping a few keys. "People often show just the highlights of their life on social media. It's common."

Harry nodded. "I know. But with Zoë, there's something more. This isn't just a travel blogger's account; it's a smokescreen. It's like she's invented this new persona. It's not the Zoë I used to know in high school. She used to despise social media and didn't care about validation from strangers."

Harry was not sure that searching Zoë's Instagram account would bring any results but still wanted to help Connor, and so she jotted down possible password ideas based on the hashtags '#BeachBlogger', '#WanderlustZoë', and '#SunsetDreamer' that accompanied several of her photos and captions. Deep down, she felt none of these would be the password they needed. The real Zoë was more complex, more layered.

As she continued scrolling through Zoë's feed, she noticed a familiar face in one of the photos. It was a selfie on the beach with the blond man, along with a few other shots. 'An epic day surfing in Koh Phangan with the best instructor ever!' If Grove followed Zoë's Instagram account, Harry was sure he would have added a like to a photo that included him. Harry wasn't wrong. There he was.

She clicked on his profile image and discovered his name was Grove Manning, a professional surfer and a native of Huntington Beach, California. Harry turned to a new page in her notepad and wrote some notes on Grove Manning. She'd go through his feed later.

Looking across the room at Connor, Harry said, "I don't believe this is Zoë's only account. I think there must be another, private one where she's her real self—an investigative reporter and independent woman who does not care what others think."

Connor considered her idea, rubbing his chin. "It's possible. People have private accounts. We might be able to find it when we log into her laptop."

"That would be great. Because all I'm seeing here is a decoy."

Connor leaned back in his chair again, rubbing his temples. "I know, but it's not easy. It's as if this laptop has multi-layered encryption, and every time I try to bypass one layer, another pops up. Someone put a lot of effort into keeping this information safe."

Harry sighed heavily, pushing away the notes she had compiled from Zoë's social media accounts. "All this work for nothing. Zoë's social media is a fortress. Everything seems to lead to a dead end. No pets, boyfriends, or close friends—she shared every minute of her life, yet nothing at all."

Before Connor could respond, a hurried knock at the door echoed through the room, followed by Euclid's urgent voice. "Harry? Connor? Are you in?"

Rising swiftly from the sofa, Harry swung the door open to find him, eyes wide and filled with unmistakable fear. Without waiting for an invitation, he thrust his phone towards Harry's face, his hands trembling.

"Euclid, slow down," Harry said, trying to calm him. "Sit first. Let me see."

After he'd shakily taken a seat, Euclid handed her the phone. With Connor looking over her shoulder, Harry attempted to make sense of the message shown on the screen.

The soft glow from Euclid's phone cast a sharp contrast in the dimly lit room. The screen displayed a short message:

Euclid! It's Sarah. I've left because I'm sick and tired of you. The last nine years have been overpowering. I've decided to start a new life. One where I feel free. Tell everyone to stop looking for me at once. I'm fine.

Harry took a moment to absorb the words. She frowned deeply, handing the phone back to Euclid. "This doesn't sound like Sarah," she commented.

"Was it sent from her phone?" Connor asked, jumping straight to the point.

Euclid shook his head. "No, Sarah's phone is currently with the police. And another strange thing," he added, pointing at the phone screen, "is that the number's hidden. There's no trace of who it's from."

Harry's instincts told her something was awry. The message seemed calculated, almost robotic—devoid of Sarah's usual warmth and vivacity. Harry was sure someone either wrote the message pretending to be Sarah or forced her friend to write it. But why would they send such a message? And what did they have to gain by it?

Connor appeared to be reading her thoughts. "It feels that whoever sent this message wants the police to stop searching for Sarah."

"What I don't understand is why she's talking about us being together for nine years. We've only been together for two," Euclid said.

Both Connor and Harry spoke in unison, "Because it's a call for help."

"Look," Harry explained. "Someone must have told Sarah to write a goodbye message so that we would stop looking for her. But in the text, she concealed the call for help, '9-1-1'."

Euclid's eyes glistened tearfully.

"She also mentions being overpowered and wanting to be free," Harry was rereading the message, looking for more clues from Sarah. "She's being kept somewhere against her will."

"I think she's being kept by local people who didn't trust their own English skills enough to write the message," Connor added. "They are not stupid. They wanted the message to sound authentic, and that's why they asked Sarah to write it, but they don't have enough language skills to figure out that she's hidden a call for help."

"Listen," Harry grasped Euclid's arm gently. "We're not going to give up. Sarah is clearly trying to communicate with us, which means she's still alive. This is a good sign."

Euclid drew strength from Harry's words. "I can't just sit back and do nothing. But if we alert the police and it goes wrong…"

Harry sighed deeply, considering their options. "Sarah's captors are clearly watching. We need to act smart, not rashly. Have you shown this message to anyone else?"

Euclid shook his head. "No. I'm tired of talking to the police. They don't seem to be doing anything. I came here as soon as I got the message."

Harry contemplated for a moment. "Let's keep this call for help between just us for now. We need a plan. I was hoping that Zoë's laptop would tell us something useful, but we've not been able to log in."

"Do you think Zoë's death is related to Sarah's disappearance?" Euclid asked desperately.

"I don't know, but it's worth exploring the possibility," Harry said cautiously, not wanting to raise Euclid's hopes.

"I'll do anything to get her back. I've searched the beach and the jungle with the police and some volunteers. It's as if she's disappeared from the face of the Earth. Why would someone take her?"

Connor pointed at the laptop. "Maybe we can find the connection if we can get into this."

Euclid took a deep breath. "I do hope you can figure it out. I'm tired of going round in circles."

Connor's analytical mind was already several steps ahead. "Have they considered that no one has found her here because she was taken offshore? Sarah was clearly on the beach because that's where her cell phone was found. She must have witnessed something she wasn't supposed to, and they took her to keep her silent."

Euclid's face paled at the implication. "But why? Why Sarah? She's just a tourist."

"Wrong place, wrong time."

Harry concurred. "It's a plausible theory, but one thing doesn't sit right with me. If she saw something so compromising that they felt the need to abduct her, why would they keep her alive?"

Connor looked thoughtful for a moment. "Maybe they believe she told someone or shared what she saw. They might keep her alive to discover what she knows and who else is involved. Or maybe they are waiting for things to cool down before they move her or... do something else."

Euclid looked between the two, struggling to process everything. "So, there are more reasons to act. We need to find her before it's too late!"

"But apart from the fact that her cell phone was left in the sand and this recent message, we have no clues," Harry summarized their predicament. "We need more information. We need to find out about any unusual boat movements the night she disappeared. I think we should talk to the local fishermen."

Connor nodded. "And we need to do it discreetly. Alerting them might put Sarah in even more danger."

As the conversation reached a natural lull, Connor stretched his limbs and sighed. "I think I need to step away for a bit. Sometimes, a fresh perspective helps. I'll take Zoë's laptop to my hut and see if I can figure it out." He glanced at Euclid. "Also, if you don't mind, I'd like to borrow your phone for a bit. I might be able to trace the origin of that message. Even if they masked the number, there are ways to dig deeper."

Euclid hesitated, looked at his phone, and then handed it over. "It would be wonderful if you could identify the number the message was sent from. Whatever it takes to find Sarah."

Harry stood up, her body showing signs of fatigue from the emotional and mental toll of her stressful day. "I feel we should continue, but I'm just too tired. I'm sorry, Euclid. Can we regroup in the morning?"

"I'm with you. I also need time to think," Connor agreed.

Even though he felt disappointed, Euclid understood that his friends needed time to rest. "Tomorrow then. And thank you, both of you. It means the world to have you on my side."

CHAPTER 17

CLOUDED MOON

The night hangs heavy around me. I am surrounded by a pitch darkness that feels thick and impenetrable, like a dense, protective blanket woven from the shadows of a cloud-covered moon. The air is sultry, typical of a Thai beach after dusk. The salt and warm whisper of distant waves are a constant companion to my solitary figure.

I let my naked footsteps fall softly on the sand, taking a predator's care to remain unheard and unseen. The marine breeze carries the scent of freedom, of escape, but also a sour tinge of frustration. All my work for nothing—the money, the Hideaway, the new identity. Everything was almost taken from me because some insufferable New York reporter wanted to selfishly advance her career.

Why couldn't she have left me alone? That nosy little cow. Always sniffing around, asking me questions, asking others about me. She thought I wouldn't notice. All I wanted was to live in peace. Live and let live. Yet, she couldn't adhere to that simple creed. Why did she care about some rich people? They wouldn't lift a finger to help her. They have so much money they don't even know how to spend it. I just helped them along. Gave them good causes. Gave meaning to their empty little lives.

Why couldn't she understand it? If she had left me alone, she'd still be alive, taking selfies and watching whale sharks. I was surprised at how easy it was to get rid of her. Perhaps she didn't think I'd go that far to cover my past and secure my future. All it took was a pretty cocktail laced with a generous dose of strychnine. No one noticed her suffocating, and when she fell to the ground, I simply walked away. Covered by foam, no one saw her pathetic convulsions. So, that was it. Good riddance! But the question remains: How did she find me here?

The realization hit me like a slap in the face. There was a flaw in my plan. If this Kessler woman could track me here, what was stopping another journalist or another would-be detective from unraveling my beautiful life-tapestry? Now, this other woman is asking questions. Were they in cahoots? They're both from New York...

It was lucky I saw her coming out of the jungle with a laptop in a plastic bag. I knew there was something fishy about her, so I followed her to her hut. I stayed behind and listened under the window as she and her 'friend' tried to break into the machine. If they had managed to hack the device, I'd have been done for. I've become too complacent, too comfortable. I need to get rid of all the evidence soon, before she uncovers the truth. And I need to silence the other two idiots. Once the dust settles, it will be time to disappear completely—perhaps to an uncharted island off Indonesia, away from prying eyes and the pesky morality of do-gooders. Start over again, but keep a low profile this time.

I reach the small fishing boat, its underside scraping violently against the sand as I tip it over with more force than necessary. Anger is a burning coal in my gut. I shove the light vessel into the welcoming arms of the sea, the water lapping eagerly at its sides. With the bag secured at the bottom of the boat, I take the oars and begin to row. Each oar stroke punctuates my internal tirade. The plans I have so carefully laid out are now being uprooted, all because she couldn't just let it be.

Out here, with only the dumb stars as witnesses, I allow myself the luxury of rage. It pours from me in silent waves, rivaling the ocean's own deep currents.

The laptop is in the bag, and the cell phone I found next to it. The laptop was the loose end, the end of Ariana's thread that could lead back to me. But not after tonight. With a grim sense of finality, I open the bag and remove the items, one by one.

First, the laptop, such a small thing to cause so much trouble. I hold it over the water, letting it dangle for a heartbeat before I release it. It sinks immediately, a stream of bubbles marking its descent into a watery oblivion. A sense of relief washes over me. Then the phone. I toss it away and watch it fall, little flickers of reflected starlight blinking as it hits the water.

"They will never find them," I whisper to the ocean, to the silent night. It is my promise, an oath sworn to the darkest of depths.

With the evidence swallowed by the sea, I row slowly back to shore. The anger in me dimming, infusing me with a cold, resolute calm. My plan has changed, but the endgame remains the same. I will not be undone by curiosity and righteousness.

Not tonight, not ever.

CHAPTER 18

THE PASSWORD

Under the soft, fresh light of the morning sun, the veranda at the Hideaway provided a picturesque view of the shimmering sea below. The gentle song of tropical birds added to the serenity of the setting. But for Euclid, peace and tranquility remained painfully elusive.

As Harry took a sip of her freshly-made mango smoothie, she turned to him, noting the dark circles under his sorrowful eyes. "Did you manage to get any rest?"

Euclid shook his head, his fingers tracing the rim of his glass. "I tried. But every time I closed my eyes, I just replayed the events of that night over and over. It's all a blur, really. Between the party, the music, and the drinking... I just can't remember much. I vaguely recall seeing Sarah wave at me in the bar and then walk away in the direction of our hut, but it must have been a dream."

Harry placed a comforting hand on his arm. "Euclid, you can't blame yourself. What happened to Sarah is not your fault. There's no way you could've predicted or prevented it."

He looked up, meeting her gaze. "I just wish I could've been there for her, you know? Protect her, or at least remember something... anything that could help us now."

She squeezed his arm reassuringly. "I know, but sometimes things happen that are beyond our control. Right now, the best thing we can do for Sarah is to stay focused, support each other, and find her."

"You're right, Harry. Thank you." He regarded his friend with a concerned frown. "You look as if you hardly slept yourself."

Harry sighed, pushing aside her smoothie, her gaze meeting Euclid's. "I couldn't," she admitted. "After you and Connor left, my mind was racing. I kept thinking about Zoë's laptop and how we might be able to break into it. I also searched the internet and social media for this guy, Grove Manning."

"Zoë's boyfriend?"

"I'm not sure if he was her boyfriend. Why would you say that?"

"I don't know. I just assumed from their body language during the shark trip."

"That's interesting. You might be right. I saw him in Zoë's photos on her Instagram, and they were dancing together at the foam party."

"Do you think he had something to do with Zoë's death? Did he take Sarah? I think we should talk to him."

"That's the problem. He checked out of the Hideaway, and his social media has been quiet since then. I have no idea where he could be. I also spoke to my grandmother. She went over to Zoë's parents' house to tell them what had happened. They are devastated."

"Did you tell them you suspect it wasn't an accident?"

Harry lowered her voice. "I was tempted to. I wanted to call them to ask them questions... I thought her mom or dad might know the password to her laptop.

But how do I explain why I need to know such personal things without alarming them? And suggesting there might be foul play... I wasn't sure I had enough evidence. Just Zoë's word that someone here was not who they claim to be."

"So, what did you do?" Euclid asked.

Harry hesitated, glancing around to ensure no one was within earshot. "I went back to Zoë's hut last night."

"Again?" Euclid's voice held a mixture of surprise and confusion.

Realizing her slip, Harry's eyes widened a fraction. "Sorry. I didn't tell you. Connor and I went there before... to look for clues."

Euclid listened attentively. Harry met his gaze steadily, an unspoken agreement of trust hanging between them. "And last night, I thought I might find something else—something we missed."

"And?" Euclid leaned forward, his earlier exhaustion momentarily forgotten in the face of this revelation.

The mischievous gleam in Harry's eyes was impossible to miss. She reached into her shorts' pocket and retrieved a Post-It note, which she held out for Euclid to see. He looked in confusion as he examined the cryptic sequence of numbers.

"What is this?" Euclid asked.

"It's got to be the password," Harry declared, her voice thick with excitement. She recounted her late-night adventure, explaining that, after scouring Zoë's hut for any clues that could help them crack the laptop, she finally turned her attention to the make-up bag. That's when she noticed something odd—a small cut in the lining that wasn't immediately apparent. Probing the incision had revealed a secret compartment and a tightly folded piece of paper within it.

"Zoë must have stashed it there in case she ever forgot the password," Harry surmised. "I do the same with my strong passwords—jot them down on a Post-It and hide them in my favorite book."

Euclid took the note and studied it for a few minutes. It read 'φ 21 4181 13 0 1 0 29'.

"It looks like a phone number to me, but why 'φ', the golden ratio... associated with the Fibonacci sequence," Euclid mused, his voice trailing off into the sound of the waves.

"If it's a phone number, we're missing the country code. I dialed it and got nowhere."

"The phi symbol makes no sense. Do you have any thoughts on why Zoë would include it?"

"I don't think it's part of the password. It would be hard to type the phi symbol on a keyboard. Still, it could be a clue."

"It makes sense, but the question is, how does it relate to these numbers? They don't follow the Fibonacci sequence." There was newfound hope in Euclid's voice and demeanor.

"We should try the numbers on her laptop and see what happens," Harry suggested, standing up. "Even if it's not the complete password, it might point us in the right direction. By the way, I'm surprised Connor didn't come down for breakfast. He must have overslept, or maybe he's already hacked the laptop and is busy reading Zoë's files. There's no time to waste."

As they made their way towards Connor's hut, the seriousness of the situation continued to bear down on them. The hut's windows and doors were closed, but they agreed they had to wake Conner up. Zoë's laptop might have information that could lead them to Sarah's whereabouts. Euclid's closed hand thudded against the door in a series of heavy, urgent knocks. The silence that followed was unsettling. With each passing second, Harry's expression twisted with worry, a knot of unease growing in her gut.

"Connor?" Euclid's voice echoed against the closed door.

"This is strange," Harry declared. "If Connor didn't come down for breakfast, he must be still in his hut. I think we should look inside."

Euclid stepped to the side to peer through the window on the porch, his breath fogging up the glass. "It's too dark... I can't see clearly."

Driven by a surge of fearful apprehension, Harry rushed to the side window and pressed her face against it, squinting to adjust her vision to the dim light inside the hut.

"Oh my God... Euclid, he's—he's in there!" Her voice was a mix of fear and shock.

They were in motion in an instant, their bodies slamming against the locked door in tandem. It burst open, revealing a disturbing scene inside.

"Connor!" Harry's scream tore through the still morning air as they stumbled into the room.

"Please, tell me you're okay!" Euclid cried out, dropping to his knees beside Connor, his hands searching desperately for a pulse.

Harry, her instincts kicking in despite the dread that filled her, reached for her phone. "I'm getting help," she declared, her voice shaking as she dialed with fingers that would barely cooperate.

While Harry spoke on the phone, Euclid held Connor's wrist, searching for a sign of life. His pulse was a weak, fading rhythm beneath his warm skin.

"He's got a pulse," Euclid announced. His eyes met Harry's, both filled with the same confusion and fear. There was no bloody wound on his body, no signs of a struggle inside the hut. In fact, there was nothing to indicate violence had occurred, yet poor Connor lay unresponsive on the floor next to his bed.

Harry relayed what she saw to the female emergency dispatcher on the telephone. After putting her on speakerphone, Harry and Euclid placed Connor in the recovery position. They checked Connor's breathing and pulse while the dispatcher provided medical advice.

Harry's mind raced, trying to piece together what could have incapacitated Connor so quickly and silently. She noticed the laptop and phone were missing—vital pieces of their investigation. Their absence was too coincidental to overlook. Someone had been here, someone who wanted to stop them.

"Do you think..." Euclid began, his voice trailing off, not wanting to complete the thought.

"I do," Harry said firmly, answering the unfinished question. "It's too precise, too timed. Whoever did this knew exactly when to strike and what to take."

Euclid nodded grimly, acknowledging the dark turn their search had taken. They were no longer simply following leads; they were apparently disrupting someone's dangerous agenda.

At that moment, the distant wail of an ambulance siren reached their ears, growing louder and more insistent as it approached. Euclid sprang to his feet, darting out of the hut and down the path, waving frantically to catch the attention of the approaching paramedics.

As they all entered the cramped hut, Euclid found himself standing flat against the wall, holding his breath as the paramedics assessed Connor's condition. They attached several electrical leads to his chest to monitor his heartbeat and placed an oxygen mask over his nose and mouth. Their hands moved with a practiced choreography.

The stretcher bearing Connor's unconscious form was hastily carried out of the hut, with Harry and Euclid following closely behind. The urgency of the paramedics' movements indicated that something was very wrong with Conner. As they reached the waiting ambulance parked on the walkway, one of them turned to Harry.

"He's had a severe allergic reaction," the paramedic said.

Harry's memory clicked into place, and she blurted out, "He mentioned he has a shellfish allergy."

The paramedic nodded. "That may have been the trigger." He gestured toward the open hut and the discarded snack on the table. "We noticed that packet of chips next to him. They contain traces of shrimp," he explained. "It's possible he didn't understand the warning on the packet since it's in Thai. He might have eaten them without realizing the danger. I'm just surprised he doesn't have an EpiPen with him."

Euclid's eyes darkened with understanding. The implications were staggering.

The paramedic continued, "We'll need to keep him under observation until he's conscious again." With that, the paramedics closed the doors to the ambulance and whisked Connor away, leaving a cloud of dust and stunned silence behind them.

Once the vehicle had faded into the distance, Harry turned to Euclid, her gaze intense and piercing. "I don't buy it," she declared flatly. "Someone's just tried to kill Connor. They knew about his allergy and used it to their advantage. They must have switched his snacks and taken away the EpiPen so that he couldn't inject himself when his throat started to swell up. That packet of chips with the shrimp warning is nothing but a diversion. I doubt Connor would have been so careless."

"I agree. It's far too convenient," Euclid said, his voice trailing off into the heavy air. "What now? Without the laptop, we're back to square one. We have no leads, no evidence."

The seriousness of the situation again bore down on them. The loss of Zoë's laptop and Euclid's cell phone was more than just a setback; it felt like the rug had been pulled from under their feet. The truth now seemed to be slipping further away.

"We'll need a new plan," Harry finally said, still determined to find Sarah and whoever was lurking in the shadows. "We're not just going to sit back and let this happen."

Euclid agreed. For a moment longer, they stood together, their resolve hardening.

"We need to return to Koh Samui," Euclid said.

"I think I know what you have in mind. Let's go. We can rent a speedboat at the harbor."

CHAPTER 19

CAPTAIN LAMAI

The speedboat skimmed over the glassy water, a sleek intruder cutting through the calm midday waters between the islands of Koh Phangan and Koh Samui. The sky above was a clear, unbroken expanse of brilliant blue, with the sun high and unyielding in its domain. Rays of sunlight danced upon the surface of the sea, turning it into a vast, shimmering expanse of speckled gold and turquoise, stretching endlessly in every direction.

Euclid's face was illuminated by the bright light, his features set in a hopeful expression. "Thank you for coming with me," he said, his voice nearly lost in the rush of wind and engine. "After everything that's happened—losing the laptop, Sarah's message—I figured we needed a different approach. Something... or rather, *someone* local who might know the area better than we do."

The boat bounced lightly on the flat, rolling swell. Harry sat comfortably on her seat; her gaze lost in the distant beauty where sky met sea. She turned to Euclid.

"Getting out into the open, chasing a new lead—it's exactly what we needed. When we found Connor, I felt like we hit a dead end. But maybe Captain Lamai can shine some light on things for us."

Euclid nodded, squinting in the high sun. "When I saved Lamai's life... I never would have thought we'd be back here now, relying on her knowledge. But she knows these waters and the islands like no one else. If Sarah was moved from Koh Phangan, I am sure Lamai would know where they might have taken her."

The boat raced across the water, catching the sun's rays. The bow spray sparkled like millions of thrown diamonds in the wake of the boat's rapid progress.

Harry brought her hands to her mouth as she felt the spray on her face and tasted salt on her lips. "Let's hope she has the answers we need," she murmured, more to herself than to Euclid.

The Koh Samui jetty was alive with the bustle of the midday traffic. Boats of all shapes and sizes rocked gently on their moorings. The occasional call of a seagull could be heard overhead, and the lively conversations of fishermen and tourists filled the air. The sharp scent of the sea mingled with the rising heat of the day. In the far distance, the serene outline of a yoga retreat sat amidst lush greenery. The peaceful outline of the buildings and surrounding gardens stood in stark contrast to the painful memories the property evoked in Harry—unwelcome memories of chaos that struck her anew at this uncertain moment in her pursuit of the truth.

Pushing aside her painful recollections, Harry and Euclid focused on the task at hand. They wove their way quickly through the marina on foot, their eyes scanning the dockside for Captain Lamai's boat. After a few minutes, they spotted her tour boat, its sides adorned with vibrant murals of local marine life.

They found Captain Lamai at the bow of the boat, busy coiling her mooring ropes into neat loops. She moved with an experienced grace, her hands sure and quick, occasionally pausing to check the tightness of a secure knot or the slack in a line.

Lamai's head snapped up at the sound of her name, and her face broke into a broad smile. "Euclid!" she exclaimed, her voice carrying over the noise of the marina. "I was so surprised when Harry sent me the message, but it's always good to see a friend—especially one who saved my life! And Harry! Wonderful to see you, too! You mentioned that it was an urgent matter. Come onboard! Let's talk."

Feeling a touch sheepish at the mention of his past heroics, Euclid explained the urgent nature of their visit. Lamai nodded in understanding, her expression turning serious as she heard of Sarah's disappearance. "Of course, I'll help you if I can," she responded. "Let's sit where it's private. And you must join me for some food! When I got your message, I asked my grandma to prepare a quick lunch for us."

Captain Lamai led them below deck into the crew mess, a cozy space filled with the mouthwatering aroma of home-cooked Thai food. As they entered, Captain Lamai gestured toward the wooden table fixed to the boat's sole. It was set out with a traditional spread.

"My grandmother made all this fresh this morning," she said proudly. "She insisted, actually. We have *pad krapow moo*—stir-fried pork with Thai basil and chilies. It's one of my favorites, very flavorful but with a bit of a kick." She pointed to a golden, fluffy dish next. "This is *kai jeow*, a Thai-style omelet. Simple, but delicious, especially with some of this jasmine rice."

She then pointed to a platter of fresh herbs and sliced cucumber. "These are to help cool down the spice if needed."

As they settled in to enjoy the meal, the boat swayed rhythmically. They were out of earshot of any passersby and safe to talk freely during their clandestine meeting. Captain Lamai passed around cold bottles of local beer, smiling as she added, "To wash it all down. Just what we need in this heat." Her hospitable demeanor was accompanied by an eager readiness to assist. Her willing attitude echoed a life well lived on these waters, where the line between rescuer and friend is often blurred.

Once Euclid explained in more detail what had happened to Sarah and Conner, Captain Lamai shared her concern. "This is terrible news," she said, her eyes earnest, reflecting a mixture of empathy and caution. "You must understand something about these paradise islands: They have two faces, two sides. Day is beautiful, peaceful. But night is a different story. It's dark and cruel. There's a lot of misery and abuse going on. Many families here rely on honest tourism: boat excursions, hiking, restaurants, but some make money by selling drugs to tourists."

"Are you saying drug smuggling is common here?" Euclid interjected.

"Yes, drug smugglers use nighttime hours. They move quickly, quietly. They have many boats and travel between islands—from one resort to another. They use young women to take the drugs to the customers and bring back the money. No one questions young women when they enter or leave a resort, you see." Lamai's tone was solemn.

"What about human trafficking?" Harry asked. "Could they have taken Sarah inland?"

Lamai's face darkened at the mention of that terrible crime. "That is also possible. The situation is very bad. Young people are taken and sold. It's horrible, but not uncommon, especially when people have no other options in life, and no one looks out for them."

Euclid's eyes were filled with concern. "If Sarah was abducted, where might they have taken her?"

"There are many secret places," Lamai admitted. "There are hundreds of little islands, archipelagos, and old harbors that no one uses anymore. There are tiny fishing villages where no one talks to the police. Places where bad people do business, no questions asked."

"Can we go to these places to see if we can find out more?" Harry's voice was firm, resolute.

Lamai's expression was serious. "We can try to check some fishing villages and small islands not far from Koh Phangan. I have some ideas. We might be lucky, but it's dangerous. These people, they don't play games. If they catch you, very bad things happen."

The reality of Lamai's words settled over them. The risks were high, but so were the stakes. They needed to proceed with great care, fully aware of how treacherous the terrain that lay ahead could be. They had to rely on Lamai's local knowledge and the bonds of their shared trust.

"I'll take you, but not in my boat—it's too noticeable. We'll take a small speedboat—it's faster. We'll go in and out, quickly. If anyone stops us, I explain that you're tourists. We keep some snorkeling masks and fins with us on the boat as a cover story."

"Whatever it takes, Lamai. We can't just sit around," Euclid announced. "At least now I feel like we're doing something to find her."

"I'll help you because I owe you my life, Euclid. But we must be careful. You—" she glanced at his dark complexion and curly, ebony hair, "—you'll stick out like a... how do you say... a sore finger?"

"A sore thumb," Euclid corrected her, but he understood Lamai's comment very well. He did stand out in a crowd in Thailand, not only because of his height but also because of his skin color.

Lamai turned to Harry. "And you, with your pink hair and white face, even worse. People notice your hair wherever you go. We must try not to be too visible. I'll get you a baseball cap or something."

Harry agreed, appreciating that Lamai wanted them to be as incognito as possible.

Lamai continued to outline her plan. "I have a friend. He has a speedboat we can use. He won't tell anyone. I know some places where smugglers live. They are quiet villages. We'll look there first."

Euclid exhaled, a mixture of anxiety and hope in his eyes. "Thank you, Lamai. Finally, it feels like we're making some real progress."

Harry's expression, however, was fraught with worry. "If we go to these villages, we're showing our hand. That could put Sarah in even more danger if the wrong people notice us looking for her."

"Still, we can't do nothing. If there's a chance of finding her, we must take it. We have to try," Euclid argued.

"You're right," Harry responded. "We can't just sit here doing nothing."

"Then we have a plan," Lamai concluded. "But remember, we must be like shadow and wind. Seen, but not noticed." She rose, her movements purposeful. "I'll arrange for the boat, and we'll leave as soon as possible."

CHAPTER 20

SPOTTED

In the dim, windowless food closet, Sarah sat on the cold teak floor, her hands bound uncomfortably behind her back. The rough texture of the ropes bit into her skin. The polished floor was adorned with intricate patterns that danced in the faint light that seeped in from under the door, but their beauty was lost on Sarah. She focused on the muffled Thai voices just beyond the door—indistinct yet ominously close.

Her sense of time had dissolved in this place of perpetual twilight. With its oppressive silence and claustrophobic air, the closet space felt like a world apart from everything she knew and loved. Despair crept into her thoughts, an uninvited shadow that clouded her hope and sense of resilience.

In a desperate attempt to escape her grim reality, Sarah's mind wandered to her apartment in Seoul. She envisioned her compact studio on the university campus, high up on the 20th floor, with panoramic views of the verdant Inwangsan Mountain and meandering Han River below. There, her world was open and free, so very unlike her current confinement.

She imagined a typical evening at home, the comforting routine of life with Euclid. The thought of savory Korean takeaway food brought forth a pang of hunger, sharpened by the tantalizing aromas drifting in from the kitchen on the other side of the closet door. She could almost taste the tangy, spicy flavors of *kimchi*, the sizzle of *bulgogi* on a hot plate, and the comforting warmth of steamed rice.

But here, in this dark room, laughter and warmth were distant memories. Sarah closed her eyes, trying to hold on to the fading images of home, normalcy, and a life that now seemed like a dream. The biting ropes, the foreign voices, the alien smells—they all conspired to bring her back to a painful reality she desperately wished to escape. But even as mordant despair threatened to engulf her mind, a spark of hope, dim yet unyielding, flickered within her youthful soul. She couldn't give up, not yet.

The sound of the main door to the cottage banging loudly set Sarah's heart racing. Voices in Thai, rapid and urgent, grew louder until they culminated in an explosion of shouting. She braced herself, unsure of what was to come. After a few intense minutes, the door to the tiny closet swung open, revealing the tall, slender boatman.

Blinking against the sudden influx of light, Sarah struggled to focus on his face. His command in broken English was direct and sharp. "Where you shoes? Where?"

Memories of her desperate bid for freedom on the beach came flooding back. "I... I lost them when I was running," she replied, her voice quivering.

Cursing under his breath, the man turned away, leaving the door open. Sarah could hear him return to the kitchen, his anger unrestrained as he confronted the other two boatmen. A vicious slap rang through the cottage, followed by a muffled apology. The atmosphere was tense, charged with fear and aggression.

After a moment, the slender man reappeared at her door, his expression dark and probing. "Young, black man—you know him?" he asked, his eyes searching hers for the truth.

The question sent a jolt of fear through Sarah. Euclid. They were asking about Euclid. Her mind raced. If she revealed her relationship with him, they might also capture him. Yet, as the man's impatience grew, she realized she couldn't risk provoking him further.

"He's my boyfriend. Euclid. He's American, too. We're just teachers. We don't know anything. Please, if you let me go, I won't say anything to anyone. Please..."

The slender man's face shifted, a calculating glint appearing in his eyes. He seemed to be weighing this new information, trying to decide what to do with it. After a moment, he slammed the door shut behind him.

Alone once again, Sarah's thoughts were filled with dreaded fear and concern. Had Euclid been captured while searching for her? The idea was unbearable. Yet, amidst the chaos of her thoughts, a glimmer of hope remained—Euclid was out there, and if anyone could find her, it was him.

CHAPTER 21

AT SUNSET

As Harry and Euclid approached the bar at Mango Moon Hideaway, the setting sun cast its typical warm glow over the scene, turning the sea into a glistening russet mirror that reflected the tranquil end of another day in paradise. However, the peace of the moment belied the turmoil within the young friends.

Euclid caught sight of Pierre and Dominique and gave them a friendly wave. The French couple beckoned them over with their usual warm and welcoming attitude. "Join us for a drink, *mes amis*," Pierre called out.

"We just heard from Somchai about Connor," Dominique said as they approached. "He's awake now, but they're keeping him in the hospital for the night." The relief in her voice was evident. "How very foolish of him to eat shrimp chips! I remember at the party, he apologized to us for not eating the crab. He said that he had a terrible allergy. It must have been a silly mistake to eat the chips."

"Well, it's good to hear that he's conscious." Harry decided not to correct the rumor that Connor ate seafood-flavored chips. "We've been really worried about him."

Settling into the chairs situated around the table, the small party was serenaded by the soft sounds of the evening surf. Dominique's curiosity was evident as she asked, "So, what have you two been doing today? Any progress on finding Sarah?"

Before Harry could kick him under the table, Euclid was sharing the details of their day. His voice was filled with hope. "We asked a friend of ours, Captain Lamai, for help. She knows these waters better than anyone. We took a speedboat to search along the coastal islands, looking for any clue that might lead us to Sarah."

"That sounds like a wise move. These islands hold many secrets," Pierre responded thoughtfully. "And... did you find anything?"

"We might have found something. On one of the beaches, I spotted a flip-flop. It looked a lot like one of Sarah's." A glimmer of hope shone in his eyes.

"It's hard to be certain, though. Those flip-flops are everywhere, and the design is pretty common," Harry said, adding a note of caution to the conversation.

"Still, we didn't want to leave any stone unturned. We took it to the police on Koh Phangan. The detective said they'll start a search on that island tomorrow morning."

Despite the potential lead, Harry couldn't shake off her skepticism, though she chose to keep her doubts to herself. Euclid's hope was something she didn't want to dampen. "Euclid was ready to go door-to-door in the nearby fishing cottages on the island right away," she continued, "but Captain Lamai advised against it."

"Why was that?" Dominique asked.

"She said that it's too risky," Euclid answered. "Some of those cottages could be hideouts for smugglers or other dangerous types. We didn't want to stumble into a situation we couldn't handle."

"Sounds like a good decision. It's best to let the police do it," Pierre agreed.

As the sun dipped lower in the sky, Mango Moon Hideaway was illuminated in pastel orange and red. At that sweet moment of transition, Reggie approached the group. "Ah, look at this sunset, my friends! Another day in paradise," he declared somewhat unconvincingly, raising his pink gin and tonic in an overly dramatic toast to the evening sky.

Dominique, barely concealing her amusement, rolled her eyes subtly at Harry, who responded with a polite smile. Reggie, however, seemed oblivious to the women's muted reaction to his presence.

Pierre, however, had noted a change in Reggie's usual manner. "You seem... how do you say... *préoccupé*, Reggie. Is everything okay?"

Sighing heavily and without invitation, Reggie took a seat next to Harry. He put a clipboard with some official papers on the table in front of them and took a sip of his drink before replying, "I've been at the police station all day. They were questioning me about the Hideaway, about the guests... It was endless."

This revelation piqued Pierre's curiosity. "But why? *Pourquoi* the police ask so many questions?"

Reggie shrugged, a hint of frustration in his voice. "Who knows? They're being very thorough, I suppose. It's all this business with the drowning at the foam party and the missing girl..." He paused, realizing that he was talking about Euclid's girlfriend. "Oops, sorry. They're being very thorough in their investigation."

"So, what are the police thinking?" Pierre's curiosity was evident.

"It's hard to tell what they're thinking. They grilled me about my past and even wanted to see our guest registry for the past year. I have to say, a lot of their questions confused me."

Dominique interjected with a voice of reason. "It's only normal that the police would want to make sure there is no ...hmmm...as you say... stone untouched."

"No stone unturned," Harry corrected her.

"Perhaps," Reggie said, unconvinced, and moved closer to the group. Lowering his voice, he confided, "I'll tell you something, but you must keep it to yourselves." The group leaned forward as one, all deeply intrigued. "While I was being interrogated, I caught a glimpse of Zoë's police file."

He paused, letting the weight of his words linger. "There's more to this than just an accident. But I can't say what—just a feeling. It looks to me like the police are still investigating her death even though they told us it was an accident."

A tense silence enveloped the group as they processed Reggie's words. Harry felt a cold shiver run down her spine. While she suspected that Zoë's death was no accident, hearing Reggie's sensationalized remarks added a new layer of certainty to her gut feeling.

"This is really horrible to hear. To think that someone here might have murdered an innocent woman," Dominique broke the silence.

"Did the police ask you about Sarah? Did they tell you anything?" Euclid was eager to find out if there was any progress in finding his girlfriend.

"They did ask me about Sarah, but I couldn't offer much help. I'm sorry, Euclid. I'd retired to bed by midnight while the party was still in full swing. I didn't see anything."

That's strange, Harry thought. She distinctly remembered Somchai telling her that Reggie went out with some guests in the early hours of the morning. *Why would he lie about it?*

"Today, while I was searching the shores of some of the other islands, I found something that might belong to Sarah," Euclid shared with Reggie. "The police are going to search that area tomorrow. I hope they find her."

Reggie's eyes widened. "Do you know what time the police are starting? We have a Full Moon Party to prepare for. I hope there won't be any disruptions."

"Not sure," Euclid said, surprised and somewhat annoyed that saving his girlfriend's life was somehow less important than Reggie preparing for a party. "They were quite clear that they didn't want me or any other civilians involved in the search."

"The detective who took our statement wasn't pleased with our discovery. It seemed like he wanted to keep us at a distance from the investigation," Harry added.

Reggie finished his drink and rose to leave. "Despite everything, the Full Moon Party is still on for tomorrow. I'm very sorry, Euclid, but we can't cancel it—people are coming here from abroad to enjoy this once-in-a-lifetime experience. It's going to be a big event. The beach below will be quite lively."

Reggie picked up his clipboard and walked away. As soon as he was out of earshot, Dominique spoke. "Did you see the piece of paper on his clipboard? It was an invoice for rat poison."

Harry's stomach turned slightly at the idea that rodents were running around the Hideaway.

"That's gross," Euclid said. "I know we're surrounded by jungle, but I hope the little creatures don't enter our huts or the restaurant."

Harry also stood up, excusing herself. "I'm sorry. I need to go," she said vaguely. She didn't want to divulge the true purpose of her late-night excursion in case it was another dead-end on her quest to find out what had happened to her parents.

CHAPTER 22

THE TRUTH

Once outside the Hideaway, Harry pulled out her phone, checking the map one last time. The location pin that Captain Lamai had sent her indicated that it was a twenty-minute scooter ride away.

On their journey back to Koh Phangan, she had shared with Lamai her frustration in trying to locate the captain of the boat that had capsized with her parents aboard. She could not believe that no one on the island remembered the incident. Captain Lamai explained that the local people knew about it very well—it's not often that foreigners die in boating accidents here. But they don't like to share their knowledge with outsiders. Lamai made a few phone calls to her friends and came up with Captain Aroon's current address, which was not too far from the Hideaway. Harry was thankful for the break in her private investigation.

The buzz of her moped broke the quiet of the night. She knew it was risky to embark on this journey in the darkness, but the need for closure, to find answers about her parents' tragic demise, had been a constant ache in her heart for nearly two decades.

The journey through the dark jungle of Koh Phangan was both exhilarating and nerve-wracking. Almost at its full phase, the bright moon cast a metalic, ethereal glow over the landscape, illuminating the winding road ahead. Tall trees and dense undergrowth flanked the paved track, their silhouettes swaying gently in the night breeze. The road twisted and turned, taking Harry deeper into the heart of the island's lush wilderness.

Finally, her navigation app announced that she had arrived at her destination. Hidden behind a screen of giant banana plants, a small wooden cottage came into view. Its rustic appearance was warm and inviting, with yellow light spilling out from the windows and onto the porch. To her surprise, she spotted a group of people lounging on hammocks outside the cottage, casually sipping bottles of beer. The scene was far from what Harry had expected.

As she killed her moped's engine, the nocturnal chorus of the jungle again settled in around the property. The calls of night owls echoed through the trees, adding to the surreal night-time atmosphere.

Harry walked up to the group, their curious gazes tracking her as she approached. "Hi, I'm Harry," she introduced herself. "I'm looking for Captain Aroon. Do any of you know him?"

A young man and woman exchanged glances then turned back to Harry. "Captain Aroon? Sorry, we haven't heard of him," the Australian woman replied in a friendly yet perplexed tone.

Harry's heart sank slightly, but she didn't lose hope. Maybe they simply hadn't crossed paths with the captain. Seeing Harry's confusion, the woman explained that they were just renting a room in this quaint cottage.

Just then, a Thai man emerged from the house, having overheard the conversation. "I think you're looking for my grandfather," he said in fluent English.

"I was given this address by Captain Lamai from Koh Samui. She told me Captain Aroon lives here," Harry explained with urgency.

The young man's smile faded slightly as he processed her words. "Yes, my grandfather lives here. He's retired now and doesn't charter boats anymore, so we don't call him 'captain' these days," he explained. Introducing himself as Pravat, he seemed puzzled. "How can I help you?"

Harry quickly clarified her true purpose. "I need to talk to your grandfather about an incident that happened twenty years ago when a boat he was captaining sank near Koh Samui."

Pravat's expression darkened. After a brief pause, he gestured towards the house. "Please come inside. This isn't something we should discuss out here," he said, leading Harry away from the curious ears of his guests.

Pravat guided Harry to a simple yet cozy living room located at the back of the property. The place felt lived in, with personal touches that spoke of a life deeply connected to the sea. He excused himself for a moment, leaving Harry alone with her thoughts. A deep sense of anticipation filled her heart as she braced herself for her conversation with Captain Aroon.

Pravat's grandfather entered the room slowly with quiet dignity. His hair was a silvery gray, and his face bore the marks of a life spent at sea. He greeted Harry with a traditional Thai gesture, his hands pressed together in a respectful *wai*.

"His English is quite basic, but I can translate for you," Pravat offered.

Harry nodded appreciatively, grateful for Pravat's assistance. She cleared her throat, gathering her thoughts before diving into the questions that had burned in her mind for years. "May I ask you about the boat that sank near Koh Samui harbor twenty years ago?" she inquired gently. "You see, my parents died in that accident, but it's never been made clear to me what exactly happened and why."

Captain Aroon nodded solemnly, a shadow of an old, guilt-ridden pain flickering in his eyes. He motioned for her to sit down on a woven rattan mat on the floor. As they settled into a more comfortable position, a middle-aged woman approached. She greeted Harry with a smile and exchanged a few words in Thai with Pravat.

"That's my mother," Pravat explained. "She's asking if you would like some *cha manao*. It's Thai iced tea."

"Yes, *kap khun*, thank you, that would be lovely," Harry responded, her heart pounding as she sat before the man who might be able to tell her what had happened so many years ago.

As the woman left to prepare the tea, Pravat turned his attention back to his grandfather. Captain Aroon began to speak in a low, steady voice. Pravat listened intently, then turned to Harry to translate the words.

"My grandfather says he remembers that day very clearly," Pravat began. "It was a day like no other, a tragedy that has stayed with him all these years." He paused, giving Harry a moment to brace herself for the story that was about to unfold.

Pravat relayed his grandfather's story, his voice growing more somber with each word. "He says there was a terrible hurricane that day. He didn't want to leave the harbor, but the ferry boat's owners insisted he go. Not long after they set out, the boat began to take on water."

Captain Aroon paused, his eyes distant as if reliving the harrowing experience. "The waves were enormous," Pravat translated. "He gave life jackets to everyone, and soon, the Coast Guard arrived to help. While the evacuation was underway, he checked the boat to ensure no one was left behind."

Pravat hesitated, glanced at his grandfather, then back to Harry. "In one of the guest cabins, he heard loud voices. My grandfather thought they needed help."

Captain Aroon's gaze lowered to the floor, a pained expression crossing his face. "He says when he looked inside, he saw a group of five people—two couples and a young woman. He remembers the young woman very well; she had a cascade of curly blonde hair. She was sitting on the floor, holding her knees and crying hysterically. She was sitting between the two couples. One of the other women was holding a gun and pointing it at the other couple on the sofa—they had their hands up. The woman with the gun was speaking to the young woman as if to calm her down. There was a lot of shouting across the cabin. It was hard to say what was going on; who was the good guy and who was the bad guy. The strange thing was that they didn't speak English to each other. My grandfather thinks it might have been Russian, but he's not sure."

"My grandfather was scared of the gun. He ran away and didn't tell the Coast Guard what he'd seen. He thought it was best not to get involved in whatever happened in that cabin."

Harry listened, her mind racing. Pravat's mother returned with the *cha manao*. The sweet, fragrant aroma of the freshly made tea was a momentary distraction from the serious conversation. Harry thanked the woman, her mind still churning with the implications of Captain Aroon's story. She pulled out her phone and asked Pravat to show his grandfather the photo of her parents. It was a lovely portrait taken on a wooden pier the summer before they died.

"He says that the man is definitely the same. He remembers the curly red hair. But the woman, he's not sure. He only saw her profile briefly. The other couple had dark hair. The woman had a dark ponytail. He saw their photos again during the trial," Pravat translated, with a heaviness in his voice.

Harry felt confused. Her mother had short, light hair. A dark ponytail did not make sense. Was it her mother who was holding the gun? Who was the other man? And what was her father doing on a boat speaking Russian?

"Why didn't your granddad call for help?"

"He regrets it now. It was the worst decision of his life. It ruined his career. But at that moment, he didn't want to risk anyone else's life, especially the members of the Coast Guard. If they had intervened in that cabin, someone innocent could have been hurt or worse," he explained.

"What happened after the boat sank?" she asked.

Captain Aroon's face was a mix of sorrow and resignation as he recounted the aftermath. "Two bodies were found in the water," Pravat relayed. "The media said they were American doctors. The headlines announced that they had drowned during the hurricane, but that's not true."

Harry felt a knot form in her stomach. This was the moment she had been waiting for; the truth about her parents.

"The photo in the coroner's report during the inquest showed that the victims were the man and woman from the cabin—the ones held at gunpoint," Pravat continued. "My grandfather believes they were shot, but this was never discussed in court."

Captain Aroon looked down. His grandson's voice was barely audible. "He was blamed for negligent homicide. He spent two years in prison and lost his captain's license. He hasn't spoken of these events since his trial, believing it too dangerous to reveal what he witnessed."

Harry's mind raced. "Do you think the others are still alive?" she asked tentatively.

Captain Aroon and Pravat exchanged a look. "It's been almost twenty years," Pravat translated. "My grandfather has no idea what happened to the other people. Once he saw the gun, he ran back on deck to the Coast Guard's boat and abandoned his boat. He only knows what he saw that day."

After finishing her tea and expressing her sincere gratitude for their hospitality, Harry reassured them that their story would remain confidential, explaining that it was for her personal closure only.

Stepping out of the cottage, Harry took a deep breath of the night air that now hosted a nocturnal cacophony of frogs and geckos. As she pondered the captain's account, she struggled to make any sense of it. Why would her parents be speaking Russian? And her mother? Holding a gun? It was all too bizarre.

Furthermore, if the victims were the other couple, then where were her parents, and what happened to the young woman? The lack of any tangible evidence or logical connection was frustrating. Harry's only hope of finding closure had led nowhere. She tried to think what her next step should be. There were no other witnesses she could question.

Mounting her moped, Harry felt she was back to where she had started, with more questions than answers. What had truly happened to her parents? These questions danced across her mind as she rode away into the night, the mystery of her parents' fate still unsolved.

CHAPTER 23

TAKEN

Although he kept his eyes closed, Euclid lay restless inside his hut, unable to succumb to sleep. His mind was consumed with worry for Sarah. The thought of returning home without her was unbearable. How could he possibly face her parents? He had met them the previous year at their home for Thanksgiving. The memory of their warm family home and the happy celebrations now twisted painfully in his heart.

He recalled how kind Sarah's parents were. Her parents, who ran their own veterinary clinic, had brought home a stray beagle that had just been diagnosed with diabetes and needed his glucose level to be checked every few hours. They hadn't wanted to leave him all alone at the clinic over the Thanksgiving holiday. When Euclid asked Sarah's dad about the dog, he told him life was about investing in others: animals, people, and communities. That gave life meaning.

Euclid now felt like a complete failure. Sarah's parents had spent decades saving multiple lives, yet he could not even look after one person. He tried desperately not to think of Sarah's death. She had to be alive. He had to bring her home. It took a long time before Euclid finally drifted off, dreaming that Sarah had returned. In his dream, he was in their apartment, and she simply walked through the main door, just as she usually did after a day at work. Putting away her keys, she asked him why he hadn't fed the cats. She was not happy that her pets were hungry. Euclid tried to explain, but he could not open his mouth.

As Euclid's eyes snapped open, a powerful hand clamped over his mouth, stifling any cry that he might make for help. It wasn't a dream anymore. Panic surged through him as he realized he was being suffocated. His heart raced, and adrenaline coursed through his veins, but he couldn't see who was in his room. Desperation took hold as he struggled against his unseen assailant, his mind racing with questions and fear.

As Euclid struggled beneath the firm grip, a familiar voice pierced the darkness, making him pause in his frantic efforts to break free. It belonged to Detective Niran, who had last spoken to him that afternoon when Euclid had given him the flip-flop he and Harry had found on the beach.

"I'll take my hand off your mouth if you promise not to shout or alarm anyone," Detective Niran commanded. Euclid, realizing that resistance would be futile, nodded in agreement.

As the hand was removed from his mouth, Euclid gasped for air. "Why are you doing this?" he asked, his voice shaky.

"I'm very sorry if I scared you," the man spoke calmly and quietly. "I've been trying to wake you gently, but nothing worked. I didn't want you to scream. No one must know that I'm here."

Euclid hesitated, confusion and apprehension colliding in his mind. "But why?" he pleaded, desperate for some understanding. "I haven't done anything."

"If you want to see your girlfriend again, you need to trust me." the detective explained, his tone leaving no room for further questioning. "That's all I can tell you right now. You must come with me, but no one must know about it."

The mention of Sarah made Euclid's heart race. Despite the bizarre and frightening situation, the possibility of finding Sarah spurred him to comply. The fact that the detective mentioned the prospect of seeing her meant that she was still alive. But if the detective knew where she was, why hadn't he brought her home? Was it some kind of a trap? Was Niran working with the gang of human traffickers or whoever took Sarah? Euclid did not have time to decide whether to trust him but he felt it was his only chance of getting closer to finding his girlfriend. He had to take this risk, however dangerous or incomprehensible it seemed. If he ended up dead at the bottom of the sea, at least he had tried.

"We need to leave the Hideaway quietly," the detective said, his voice a strange mixture of sternness and reassurance. "No one must see us. A car is waiting for us outside. Take your backpacks, too."

Euclid put on a pair of tracksuit pants and a hoodie. As he tied his shoelaces, he couldn't help but wonder if he had made the right decision. There was still time to run or call for help. Was he being abducted? He had heard of criminals working in cahoots with the police. Was Detective Niran corrupt? Did the discovery of Sarah's footwear put her and Euclid in danger? But the thought of Sarah, possibly in danger and needing him, kept him silent and cooperative, even as the unknown loomed ahead. Euclid knew that if he didn't follow this last lead, he might have to return home and face Sarah's parents. They would never forgive him. He would never forgive himself.

CHAPTER 24

PARTY PREPARATIONS

S tepping out onto her porch, Harry was greeted by the warmth of the tropical sun. The panoramic view of the open sea never ceased to amaze her, and it offered her a brief relief from the turmoil of recent events.

She stretched her arms upward, feeling the tension in her back and neck muscles ease slightly. The past few days had been a whirlwind of confusion, fear, and sleepless nights, fueled by her relentless pursuit of the truth behind Zoë's death, Sarah's disappearance, and her parents' fate. The emotional and physical toll had finally caught up with her, resulting in restless nights.

As she descended the steps of her hut, Harry's thoughts turned to the police search. She hoped that the flip-flop Euclid had found might lead to some tangible clues about Sarah's whereabouts. Despite her eagerness to check in on him, she knew it was wise to give Euclid some space, especially after the intense experiences they had shared the day before.

Harry set off for a solitary walk along the beach. The rhythmic sound of the waves crashing against the shore and the feel of the soft sand beneath her feet would calm her spirit. She needed this time alone to process her thoughts and maybe, just maybe, come up with a new angle to approach the baffling mystery that had entangled her and her friends on this paradise island. Suddenly, she guiltily remembered that Connor was being discharged from the hospital that morning. She pulled out her phone and sent him a message.

Harry: Hi. Heard that you're getting released from the hospital today. When are you getting here? We need to talk.

Connor: Are you joking? I'm not coming back after what happened. Sorry.

Harry: Shall we meet in town?

Connor: Yes. Can you bring my backpack, please?

Harry: Anything else?

Connor: Zoë's laptop?

Harry: It's gone.

Connor: That's what I thought. Meet you at 2 in the Irish Pub opposite the harbor. You can't miss it. It's called Tropical Murphy's.

Harry: OK

Connor: Don't tell anyone you spoke to me.

After confirming the message, Harry deleted the exchange and pocketed her phone. As she walked down the last of the wooden steps, she was taken aback by all the commotion on the beach. The Mango Moon Hideaway staff were bustling around in preparation for the Full Moon Party, a significant function that drew a large crowd to the resort every month. Despite the recent unsettling events, the atmosphere was one of excitement and anticipation. The guests and staff did not seem affected by Zoë's death or Sarah's disappearance.

Some workers were constructing a giant fire pit near the shoreline, which would later become the heart of the evening's festivities. Its size suggested it would be quite a spectacle once lit, creating a focal point for the party-goers.

Sets of tables and chairs were being arranged on the sand, forming a semi-circle a safe distance from the fire pit. Each table was adorned with colorful tablecloths, and strings of colored lanterns were being hung from poles set in the sand, ready to illuminate the beach with a soft, ambient light when darkness fell.

In one area of the beach, about 40 meters from the fire, a small stage was being set up, presumably for a live music set or a DJ. The sound system was already in place, with workers carefully testing each speaker to ensure the music would carry over the sound of the waves and the chatter of the crowds.

Harry watched for a moment longer as Reggie and Somchai engaged in what appeared to be a heated discussion near the stage. Reggie's arms flailed with frustration while Somchai maintained a calm, almost stoic demeanor, absorbing her manager's apparent barrage of complaints with a patience that seemed almost otherworldly.

Harry checked her phone and noted it was already noon. She had only two hours to gather Connor's belongings for their meeting. The thought of breaking into his hut made her uneasy.

Decision made, Harry headed towards Somchai, who noticed her approach and excused herself from her conversation with Reggie. As she walked away, Reggie's animated expressions ceased and were replaced by a sullen quietness.

"Somchai, I need to pick up some things from Connor's hut. He's getting out of the hospital today and won't be coming back. Could I get the key, please?"

"I'm so happy he's feeling better. It was such an unfortunate incident. So silly of him. Let's get the key."

Harry followed the receptionist to the main office.

"Do you need a ride to take his luggage to the hospital?"

As Harry assured Somchai that she could manage on her moped with Connor's backpack, Somchai's attention shifted to the upcoming Full Moon Party.

"Will you be joining us tonight, Harry?" she inquired, her expression brightening at the idea. "It might take your mind off recent events."

"I'll try," Harry replied, her mind still partly occupied with her upcoming meeting with Connor.

"You really should. It's quite a party," she said excitedly. "Guests will start arriving in the afternoon, but it really comes alive at night. I'd say it's a once-in-a-lifetime experience. It will be great for your blog."

Harry smiled, appreciating Somchai's enthusiasm. "I'll try to make it back in time," she promised. Even though, with the stress and trauma of the past few days, she really didn't feel like joining in. She also remembered Zoë telling her that something was going to happen during the event. She had spoken of a setup or sting to catch the imposter. Harry wasn't sure if the trap had been set by Zoë or if there were other people involved, but it might be worth going to the party to see what happens. There was a chance that whoever killed Zoë would be there too, unaware that Harry was on their trail.

After saying 'thank you' for the key at the reception, Harry set off towards Connor's hut. The backpack wouldn't be too cumbersome to carry on her moped, and she felt eager to meet Connor after his ordeal. Despite the festive atmosphere that was building up around the resort, her thoughts remained focused on the more pressing matter at hand.

CHAPTER 25

THE LUCK OF THE IRISH

Harry's moped buzzed along the bustling streets of Thong Sala, the gateway town to the island of Koh Phangan. Vibrant colors and cheerful sounds enveloped her as she navigated through the throngs of people and vendors lining the main road. The lunch-time air was rich with the aromas of street food: the sweet scent of grilled pineapple on bamboo sticks, the spicy fragrance of *pad thai* being stir-fried in large woks, and the tantalizing smell of skewered meats sizzling over charcoal fires. Vendors called out to passing tourists, their high-pitched voices mingling with the clatter of pots and pans.

The sea, a stunning shade of turquoise at this time of day, provided a picturesque backdrop to the fishing boats that bobbed gently on their moorings in the harbor. Strong-armed fishermen could be seen hauling in their morning catch, adding to the town's lively atmosphere. The essence of the sea mixed with the salty breeze brought a feeling of welcome freshness to the air that hovered over the island.

As Harry approached the harbor at the heart of Thong Sala, she encountered the bustling street market. The narrow lane was now packed with people, forcing her to disembark from her moped and push it through the crowd. The market was a kaleidoscope of colors and textures, with stalls overflowing with various goods. She saw intricate handicrafts for sale, from hand-woven baskets to delicately carved wooden figures. They were all beautiful items showcasing local artisans' skills and craftsmanship. She also spotted many clothing stalls displaying racks of flamboyant sarongs, tie-dye shirts, and hand-stitched dresses, their patterns inspired by traditional Thai designs.

The voices of the Thai vendors rose above the crowd, each trying to outdo the other in attracting the attention of the passing hordes of tourists. These eager entrepreneurs touted their wares enthusiastically, offering handmade jewelry, colorful lanterns, and exotic spices to everyone who passed by their stalls. The market's energy was infectious, and the blend of locals and tourists created a lively, communal atmosphere.

After navigating through the market, Harry finally entered the harbor area. The Irish pub, just as Connor had described, was indeed impossible to miss. Adorned with green shamrocks, it stood out among the other local establishments.

Is there an Irish pub in every town in the world? Harry mused to herself as she parked her moped outside.

Stepping into the bar area, she was greeted by the familiar sound of Irish folk music. The walls were decked with posters of Irish landscapes, Irish street signs, and various pieces of period memorabilia, creating an intimate atmosphere. It felt like a little piece of Ireland had been miraculously dropped into this far-flung corner of the world.

She quickly spotted Connor sitting at the bar, a half-empty pint of Guinness in front of him. A sports channel on the large TV screens fixed to each wall seemed to have captured the attention of most of the patrons, their reactions ranging from overly excited cheers to despondent groans at the live football match being broadcast.

"Connor! It's so good to see you," Harry said, greeting him, a smile belying her concern. She placed his backpack next to his stool and sat beside him. "And in an Irish setting like this one."

"My nerves are shattered, to be honest. I needed a touch of familiarity, something from home to calm me down."

The bartender, noticing a new customer, approached the young couple with a friendly demeanor. "Would you folks like something to eat? Our homemade sausage rolls are quite popular," he suggested.

"Sure, we'll share a plate of those, thank you," Harry replied.

As the bartender walked away to place their order at the kitchen hatchway, Harry turned her full attention back to Connor. They needed to catch up and strategize their next move, especially given the recent turn of events.

The relaxed atmosphere of the pub, combined with the comforting smell of freshly baked food, provided a temporary respite from the commercial chaos that reigned outside.

As soon as the friendly bartender was out of earshot, Harry asked Connor why he had eaten shrimp chips when he knew he was allergic to them. Connor shook his head, clearly frustrated.

"I didn't eat any shrimp crisps. I had a packet of normal potato crisps in me hut. I opened it the day before and didn't finish them. Someone must have slipped a few shrimp crisps inside it."

Harry's expression turned grave as she processed this.

"So, you think someone tried to kill you? To stop you from finding out what was on Zoë's laptop? But the police found a bag of *shrimp* chips on your night table."

Connor nodded, his face set in a determined frown.

"Exactly. When I started to choke, I couldn't find my EpiPen. Whoever tried to kill me must have taken it to ensure I suffocated. They must have watched me from outside my hut, and when I passed out, they must have swapped the bags to suggest I was a total idiot who fed himself shrimp. I'm sure of it. I'm leaving the island, Harry. It's too dangerous here."

Connor then picked up a miniature sausage roll and inspected it briefly before popping it into his mouth. "Mmm! These sausage rolls are bangin'," he commented once he had swallowed one. "Just like in Dublin."

"But what about our investigation?" Harry asked, a little annoyed that he was paying more attention to the sausage rolls than to the serious issue at hand. "We need to find out who killed Zoë. And even more importantly, we need to find Sarah!"

Connor looked torn. "I understand the stakes, Harry, but after this close call, I can't risk staying. I'll help from a distance. But here, on this island, it's too risky. It's just as Zoë told you. There's a ruthless snake at the Hideaway. They'll kill whoever tries to stop them." He helped himself to another sausage roll.

Harry understood his fear and reluctantly accepted his decision. She knew the danger was real, but she also knew they couldn't give up. With or without Connor on the island, they had to keep pushing forward.

"So, what are your plans now?"

Connor took a slow sip of his Guinness before replying. "I've rented a small place on Koh Tao. The island is not far from here. It's quieter there. I'm catching the ferry in an hour. I really don't see how we can find out who Zoë was investigating without her laptop," he explained matter-of-factly. "By the way, did you check if my laptop is in my backpack?"

Harry shook her head. When she had collected his clothes and personal items from his hut, she had simply jammed them in his backpack without paying attention to what was already inside it.

Connor jumped off his stool and opened his backpack, fishing a thin laptop out from the bottom. "Phew! I thought they took mine, too. I changed my cloud password as soon as I woke up in the hospital."

Harry went silent for a few seconds as Connor's words made her think of something she hadn't considered before.

"That's it, Connor! You're a genius! We need to access her cloud. I mean, most of my work, my photos, and blog posts are in the cloud. Zoë must have done the same. She'd have made a backup of her documents there."

Connor set down his pint, considering. "You're right. I don't know why I didn't think of it before. Sometimes, when you focus on one solution, you stop seeing the forest for the trees. Yet, we still need the password. It will be tough without it. We also need her email address."

"Well, I have that on my phone, in my contacts," Harry explained, her eyes lighting up with the spark of an idea. "And I think I know her password."

Connor looked at her with a mix of surprise and intrigue. "How did you...?"

Harry explained how she found the Post-It in Zoë's hut

Connor's eyes narrowed as he looked at a photo of the Post-It note on Harry's phone. "Are these numbers her password?"

Harry, with a spark of inspiration, explained her theory to Connor. "I don't think it's these numbers. I think the password might be an alphabet code based on the Fibonacci sequence. Euclid explained it to me yesterday. Each number would correspond to a letter of the alphabet by following the sequence."

Seeing Connor's confusion, she requested a piece of paper and a pen from the bartender, who handed her a notepad. On it, Harry began writing down the first 26 numbers of the Fibonacci sequence, associating each with a letter from the alphabet. "It starts with 0, 1, and then each subsequent number is the sum of the previous two."

"I know," Connor said, familiar with the concept.

Carefully, she wrote the letters of the alphabet next to their Fibonacci counterparts:

0 - A

1 - B

1 - C

2 - D

3 - E

5 - F

8 - G

13 - H

21 - I

"So, I matched these numbers and got this. Look!"

Next, she matched each number with a letter:

21 - I

4181 - T

13 - H

0 - A

1 - B / C

0 - A

"Ithaba?" Connor read.

"No, silly. It's Ithaca, our hometown."

Harry looked up at Connor with anticipation. "So, if we've got this right, Zoë's password is 'Ithaca29' since, as I discovered last night, the number 29 is not part of the sequence."

Connor, intrigued by the ingenuity of the approach, nodded. "It's a clever system. That might work. I might be able to get into her cloud storage."

"In full disclosure, I've tried to access her email with this same password to see if I could find any clues, but it asked me for a verification code, so I abandoned my efforts. I didn't want the system to lock us out completely."

"That was good thinking, Harry. I have some tricks up my sleeve. I might be able to bypass the verification step," Connor said with a renewed enthusiasm. "I'll get on it as soon as I get to Koh Tao. I'll text you if I'm successful," he promised. "If I can access Zoë's cloud storage, I'll send you a link to a secret cloud location where I'll keep a copy of her files until we figure out our next move."

"Let's just hope it does the trick and that Zoë used her work email to store her research files," Harry said, relieved that she had Connor back on track. While their plan remained uncertain, they felt it was their best chance.

"Also, while you're working your magic on your laptop, can you find anything about this guy Zoë used to hang out with at the Hideaway? His name is Grove Manning. I'll text you his Instagram profile. He's kind of disappeared from social media since her death."

"Okey-dokey. I'll look for him."

Glancing at his phone, Connor realized it was time for him to leave. He downed the remainder of his beer, stood up, and took a deep breath, ready to face the next challenge. Harry, ever the supportive ally, offered to walk him to his ferry boat. As they stepped out of the quiet pub and made their way to the harbor, the hustle and bustle of Koh Phangan enveloped them once again.

The harbor was still full of activity. Tourists scurried about, boarding various boats that promised unforgettable sea adventures. Local vendors hawked their wares, adding to the cacophony that filled the air. The sky remained a brilliant blue.

Amidst this lively scene, the local ferry, packed with party-goers for the Full Moon Party, was just arriving. Its deck was awash with bright, excited faces, all eager to join the legendary festivities of Koh Phangan. The contrast between the departing and arriving crowds was stark—while some sought the tranquility of quieter islands like Koh Tao, others were drawn to the magnetic energy of the Full Moon Party.

Harry, watching the lively scene, couldn't help but comment to Connor, "Looks like there's a lot more people coming to Koh Phangan than leaving. Your ferry to Koh Tao might be a bit lonely."

Connor gave a wry smile. "I guess I'm going against the flow. But a bit of peace and quiet might be just what I need."

They reached the terminal, and Connor quickly boarded the sturdy vessel. Harry waved him off, watching as the ferry slowly departed. Her thoughts consisted of a mix of worry and hope.

"Good luck, Connor," she whispered to herself, turning away from the harbor. The Full Moon Party was gearing up, but her mind was focused on more serious matters.

Harry was about to head back to the Hideaway when a familiar figure caught her eye. A small woman with a round, friendly face was smiling at her. It took Harry a moment to place her—it was Pravat's mother, the kind lady who had served her iced tea at her home the night before.

"Hello," Harry greeted her, surprised by the unexpected encounter.

"*Sawasdee kha*," the woman replied. "You have two minute, please?"

They stepped aside, moving away from the flow of people to a quieter spot. The mother's English was basic but intelligible, and her expression was earnest.

"I know my father's story not make much sense to you," she began, her eyes meeting Harry's with sincerity. "But I want tell you, it's true."

Harry listened, intrigued. She nodded, encouraging the woman to continue.

"The night of the storm, when the boat sink, it change our lives. My father... he was never the same after that. What he saw... what happen on that boat—it is a ghost for him all these many years. He still dream about that accident and wake up shouting."

She paused, taking a deep breath as if gathering strength to share something deeply personal.

"He never talk about it, not to anyone. Not even to me. But I knew something terrible happen. Something more than sinking his boat."

Pravat's mother's voice held a steady cadence, her words carrying the sorrow of a long-kept secret. "When my father was at magistrate court for trial, it was only my mother and me at home. We worry too much. We don't know what happen to our family," she recounted, her gaze distant as if visualizing the scene from years ago. "I planned to study in Bangkok, but after the court trial, I stay here and help my mother."

"I'm sorry to hear that."

"That's okay. We all make sacrifices sometimes. One night, we were already sleeping, when suddenly, our dog barking very angry outside. My mother take a flashlight and go check. She tell me stay in my bedroom. But I am question and afraid, look through window from first floor."

She paused for a moment, collecting her thoughts before continuing. "I saw two Western men in smart suits. They come to our house in big, too expensive 4x4—I never saw a car like that in the middle of the jungle. I don't hear what they say, but I watch my mother talk them. She seemed worried, afraid."

Harry listened intently.

"The men give my mother a big paper envelope. I remember her hands shake when she took it. They speak for more minutes. My mother nod her head now and then. Then the men go quickly, same as they come."

Harry's mind raced with questions. Who were these men? What was in the envelope? Was it a bribe, a threat, or something else entirely?

"That night, after the men left, my mother come my room. Her hands still shaking," she recounted, her voice a quiet whisper. "She said she have a secret and I promise never speak about it to anyone."

Her eyes seemed to glaze over with the memory as she continued. "We opened the envelope together. It filled with hundred-dollar bills—too much money, more than my parents ever dream of in their lifetime."

Harry listened, struggling at first to make sense of this revelation.

"We put the money into small packets and hide them in secret spots around the house. I never ask my mother about it. I respect her and my father's secret."

"But last night," she continued, her voice gaining a new edge of understanding, "when I hear my father tell his story to you, I think I understand. They give money to keep my father not speak about what he saw on the boat. It was money to buy him not speak. One of the people must see him. They come when he is in jail to keep everyone quiet."

Harry nodded, absorbing every detail. "And your family's life changed after that?"

"Yes," Pravat's mother confirmed. "After my father come back from prison, we moved to a house away from the town. My parents buy a large land to farm. That money... it changed our lives."

"Thank you for trusting me with this information."

"I think you must know this. It can be important what you are looking for. It's twenty years. I don't think the men who give my family the money care anymore. It's an old story."

Pravat's mother appeared thoughtful for a moment, as if debating with herself whether to divulge more. Then, with a slight hesitancy in her voice, she spoke up. "One more thing... I don't know if it important or just a chance," she began, her tone laced with uncertainty.

Harry nodded in anticipation.

"My father speak the young woman he see on the boat has curly yellow hair," Pravat's mom continued. "I don't know if the same, but such hair is not common here. There's a Russian woman with curly yellow hair. She live on Koh Tao, the next island. Her name Olga, but everyone call 'Crazy Russian', or 'Crazy Olga'."

Harry's pulse quickened. Could this woman be the same young person that Captain Aroon saw with her parents? It was true that curly blonde hair was not particularly common anywhere in the world, and here in Thailand, it would stand out.

Pravat's mom seemed to read Harry's thoughts. "Maybe it nothing. You know, there many young Russian women around here. But Olga... she here for a very long time."

"How can I find her?" Harry asked.

"They know her on Koh Tao. Everyone know Crazy Olga. She's like a local person there," Pravat's mom replied.

Harry quickly pulled out her phone and typed in 'Crazy Olga, Koh Tao' into her notes, ensuring she wouldn't forget this potentially vital piece of information.

"Thank you so much," Harry said with gratitude. "I'll try to meet her."

As they parted ways, Harry felt a surge of hope mixed with apprehension. The Russian-speaking woman, who might have been on the same boat with her parents, could not be ignored. It was a lead she had to pursue, no matter how slim it might seem. The nickname 'Crazy Olga' echoed in her mind as she walked back to her moped.

CHAPTER 26

IN THE DARK

In the cell's darkness, Euclid felt his isolation was slowly forcing him to disconnect with the world. The small, padded room, devoid of windows, seemed more like a space designed for solitary confinement than anything else. He sat there on the cold, hard concrete bed, enveloped in an eerie and unsettling absolute silence. The lack of light and sound created an environment that confused his senses, leaving him disoriented and lost in a timeless void.

His mind raced with questions and fears. Why had the detectives, who promised him a reunion with Sarah, brought him to this lonely cell instead? The memories of being ushered out of his hut, packing both his and Sarah's belongings under the guise of cooperation, haunted him. He had believed, perhaps naively, that compliance would lead him to her. But now, in this dark, lonely chamber, doubt and fear gnawed at him.

Was he a suspect in Sarah's disappearance? Had they discovered something incriminating? Or worse, had they found her body? The thought sent shivers down his spine. The notion of being framed for a crime he did not commit and being powerless to prove his innocence was terrifying. He tried to piece together the events that had occurred since her disappearance to find some logic in this bizarre situation, but nothing made sense. Time seemed to stretch endlessly in the darkness. He had no way of knowing how many hours had passed since he had been locked up.

Suddenly, there was a faint knock on the cell's metal door. The sound was so unexpected that Euclid jerked upright, his heart pounding. He was on the verge of panic. A slit appeared near the top of the door, casting a thin bead of yellow, insipid light into the room. It was the first sign of life he had encountered since being imprisoned in this bleak space. Euclid moved closer to the opening, his heart racing with pitiful hope and apprehension. The sliver of light felt like a lifeline in the overwhelming darkness.

Euclid saw the face of the detective who had escorted him from his hut.

"Are you okay?" Detective Niran enquired, his tone surprisingly gentle given the circumstances.

"This isn't right," Euclid protested, his voice a blend of anger and desperation. "You can't just keep me here. I'm an American citizen, and I demand to see a lawyer!"

The detective listened to Euclid's outburst with a patience that seemed out of place. "You need to be quiet," he finally said. "You don't understand how serious your situation is."

"Then explain it to me!" Euclid shot back, frustration boiling in his voice. "Why am I here? What's going on? Where is Sarah?"

The detective looked at him thoughtfully as if deciding something significant. "I'll explain everything in a moment," he said, his tone grave. "But you must first promise me you'll stay silent and control your emotions."

The policeman's words only deepened Euclid's confusion and apprehension. What could possibly warrant such a warning? His heart raced as the detective unlocked the heavy metal door of his cell.

As the door swung open, Euclid's breath caught in his throat. There, in the dim light of the hallway, stood Sarah. She looked exhausted and disheveled, her clothes dirty and her hair a mess, but it was unmistakably her. A faint smile graced her lips, a sign of recognition and relief, but she quickly raised her index finger to her lips, urging him not to speak.

Sarah and the detective stepped into the now dimly lit cell. Detective Niran subtly averted his gaze, allowing Sarah and Euclid a sweet moment of private reunion amidst the chaos of their current reality. The sight of each other was a balm to their frayed nerves, and tears cascaded down Sarah's cheeks as she clung to Euclid, her voice trembling with emotion.

"I thought I'd never see you again," she whispered.

After a few moments of their shared relief and loving assurances, the detective cleared his throat, signaling his intention to proceed. He motioned for them to sit on the bed, his expression serious.

"I need to ask you both some questions," he began, his tone firm yet not unkind. "It's very important that you answer truthfully."

Euclid and Sarah, still holding each other's hands for comfort, nodded their understanding. They were ready to cooperate.

The detective's first question was directed at Sarah. "How did you end up on that boat with the gang?" he asked, his eyes keenly observing her reaction.

Sarah took a deep breath, her mind piecing together the fragmented memories of that fateful night. "I don't remember much," she admitted, her voice barely above a whisper. "I had too many cocktails and must have lost track of time. I was tired and ended up on the beach, and that's where I saw the boat. It looked more comfortable than lying on the sand, so I decided to lie down inside it and look up at the stars. I covered myself with a blanket that was on the bench there. I must have fallen asleep. The next thing I knew, I was out at sea, surrounded by strangers."

She paused, her eyes reflecting the memories. "At first, they thought I was part of their gang because of my Asian appearance. But when we got to the shore, I tried to escape, and they realized I was not one of them. When they saw the news... the search for me and the appeal for information, they got scared. They didn't know what to do with me, so they locked me up in a closet."

Euclid's heart ached for what Sarah had endured. The detective remained silent, processing Sarah's account before moving on to his next line of questioning.

"And how did you know where to look for her?" Niran asked Euclid with a hint of skepticism in his voice.

"Honestly, I didn't. We searched dozens of little islands and fishing villages with a local captain. We were just trying to find any trace of her."

The detective gave a disbelieving shrug. "So, through ignorance and bad luck, you stumbled into the operations of a dangerous gang involved in drug dealing." His tone was matter-of-fact, outlining the perilous reality of their situation. "You were very lucky that there was an undercover agent in the group. He informed us of Sarah's presence after he saw you on the news, but we had to act cautiously."

Sarah felt grateful. She explained that if it weren't for the undercover agent, she would have been dead.

"Once the gang leader saw Euclid on the beach, he realized the police might get involved and discover their hideout," she said. "He was furious. He ordered one of the boatmen to take me out to sea and... throw me overboard, with my hands and feet bound."

Euclid's heart skipped a beat, horror washing over him at the thought of what could have happened.

"But," Sarah continued, her voice steadying, "when we were out at sea, I begged and pleaded with the boatman. And then I realized he wasn't following the orders. He was actually taking me back to Koh Phangan."

The detective interjected at this point, confirming Sarah's story. "That's right. We received a coded message from our undercover agent indicating he was bringing her back. We retrieved her this morning at our usual meeting spot out at sea without attracting any attention to the handover. The boatman has since returned to the gang. Now you understand why you both must be kept out of sight. If the gang hears that Sarah is still alive, then our agent will be in grave danger."

He paused, letting the gravity of their situation sink in. "Tonight's Full Moon Party is the gang's busiest night of the month. It's when they do most of their illegal activities, under the cover of the celebration."

Euclid and Sarah exchanged a look of relief mixed with fear, realizing how close they had come to a tragic end and how dangerous the web they had unwittingly entangled themselves in was. The detective's revelation about the Full Moon Party also made them realize the enormity of the criminal activities happening right under their noses.

"For your safety and our agent's, you must remain hidden until the sting operation concludes tonight," the detective began, his tone intense yet laced with concern. "And even after that, I strongly advise that you leave the island as soon as possible. Sarah, you've been on the news. It's too risky for you to stay here."

Sarah and Euclid exchanged worried glances, the reality of their situation sinking in. The detective's insistence on their immediate departure underscored the danger they were in.

"I don't trust anyone in this matter," the detective continued. "You'll stay here, in this cell, until I'm certain it's safe for you to leave. I'll do my best to bring you some water and sandwiches."

Euclid nodded, understanding the precariousness of their position. "We appreciate your help, detective," he said, his voice a mix of gratitude and anxiety.

The detective held their gaze for a moment longer, ensuring his message was clear. "Remember, there will be no official record of you ever being here. For your own safety, you should never return to these islands."

THE FULL MOON PARTY

Evening was just about to fall when Harry arrived back at Mango Moon Hideaway. She maneuvered her scooter into a spot next to a row of other parked bikes that was noticeably longer than usual. It was clear that the Full Moon Party had attracted many guests from far beyond the confines of the resort. The deep, rhythmic bass of electronic house music reverberated through the dense jungle.

As she walked past the reception, the ever-friendly Somchai offered a quick wave, but her attention was clearly divided among several tasks, indicative of the night's busy schedule. With a sense of purpose, Harry headed straight for Euclid's hut, the thumping music growing louder with each step, almost in sync with her increasing heartbeat.

But upon reaching his hut, she found it empty. With no sign of Euclid, Harry assumed he must have joined the festivities; the overpowering music would have made staying in the hut an exercise in futility.

Approaching the wooden stairs leading down to the beach, Harry paused to take in the breathtaking scene. The sun, now just a crimson sliver on the horizon, bathed the landscape in the last dying light of the day. It was a typical Full Moon Party scene, yet it was mesmerizing in its own unique way.

The beach was alive with youthful energy and color. Throngs of people danced on the sand, their lithe bodies moving freely to the pulsating electronic beats that dominated the soundscape. Neon lights and colorful lanterns, strung up between provisionally erected poles and the palm trees, cast a surreal glow over the revelers, turning the beach into a medley of color.

Makeshift drink bars and food stalls lined the periphery of the party area, their lanterns and twinkling fairy lights adding to the enchanting atmosphere. The aroma of grilled seafood and spicy stir-fry filled the air, enticing party-goers with the promise of a delicious, impromptu meal.

In the midst of it all, small groups of dynamic fire dancers performed daring routines, their swirling movements creating captivating streaking patterns of light against the darkening sky. The crowd around them cheered and clapped, caught up in the spectacle of skill and flame.

Despite the allure of the party, Harry's mind couldn't fully detach itself from her purpose. She scanned the crowd for Euclid, her eyes darting between dancing silhouettes and illuminated faces, hoping to catch a glimpse of her friend amidst the sea of party-goers. As the very last rays of the sun dipped below the horizon, Harry stepped forward, descending the stairs into the heart of the celebration, determined to find her friend to update him on what she and Connor had decided to do.

Navigating through the festive chaos, she spotted Pierre and Dominique amidst the revelry, their figures illuminated by the flickering party lights. Pierre was sharing a joke with Dominique as they enjoyed grilled seafood snacks served on paper plates.

"Hey, have you guys seen Euclid around today?" she asked, pitching her voice high over the pulsating music.

Pierre shook his head, a hint of garlic and lemon wafting from his plate.

"*Non*, Harry, we've been hiking all day. We just got here and are *so* hungry," he replied.

Dominique added, "Yeah, we missed most of the afternoon's fun, I guess."

Pierre extended his plate towards Harry. "You must try this, *c'est délicieux!*"

Harry smiled. "Thanks, but I'll pass. This noise is something else, huh?" She gestured at the sea of dancing figures around them.

Pierre then leaned in closer to Harry's ear. "You know, it is *bizarre*, but I swear, the policeman who was here when they discovered Zoë, he's here too. Over there, dancing with a glow stick, no? He looks like he is enjoying himself very much!"

Harry squinted in the direction he pointed. "Really? It's so hard to see with these lights, and... well, it's getting dark."

Their conversation was abruptly interrupted as more party-goers arrived by speedboat, beaching themselves in the shallow water right near the party's edge, their engines' roar briefly louder than the pounding music.

As soon as the engines were cut off, Harry noticed a strange sound blending with the music. It came in sharp, relentless bursts, each one slicing through the air like a piercing scream, completely at odds with the melody.

Suddenly, a clear shout was heard across the crowd. "Fire!"

The amassed party-goers' initial reaction was one of excitement, mistaking the call for fire as part of the party's theatrics. But Harry's gaze followed the direction of the shout. She saw a terrifying glow and smoke billowing from the Hideaway's reception area up on the cliff.

Pierre didn't hesitate. His past as a firefighter kicked in. He ran to the DJ console and moved the operator to the side. "Everyone, stay by the water! Do not go towards the resort!" he bellowed into the microphone after shutting off the music.

Harry watched, stunned, as Pierre sprinted towards the danger. She turned to Dominique. "We should help, right?"

Despite Pierre's protests, they both raced after him, their feet pounding against the sandy ground. They weaved through clusters of huts and saw that the fire was rapidly engulfing the reception and the offices. The air was thick with noxious smoke and the crackling of flames, creating a terrible contrast to the festive atmosphere they had just left behind on the beach.

Pierre turned to Harry and Dominique as they neared the fiery scene. "Harry, call the fire department, now!" he instructed urgently.

He swiftly grabbed an abandoned beach towel from a nearby sun lounger, dipped it in the pool, wrapped it around his face as an impromptu mask, and charged towards the blazing office. "There might be people inside. I have to check," he called over his shoulder, his voice muffled.

Her fingers trembling with adrenaline, Harry dialed the island's emergency number. She relayed the location of the fire with as much composure as she could muster, her eyes never leaving the fierce dance of flames.

Meanwhile, Dominique, unable to stand idly by, scoured the immediate area for a water hose. Finding one coiled near a garden bed, she turned it on and dragged it towards the burning building. The hose hissed into life, sending a weak but steady stream of water towards the flames.

Harry, noticing Dominique's proximity to the fire, shouted a warning. "Dominique, be careful of the smoke!"

But Dominique was resolute. "I can't just watch. I have to do something," she yelled back, her voice laced with fear and determination.

Just as Harry was about to pocket her phone and join Dominique, a notification flashed on the screen. It was an email from Connor. For a split second, she was torn between the urgent chaos unfolding around her and her keenness to discover the contents of Connor's message. But the rising heat and the sound of crackling flames snapped her attention back to the harrowing reality she was confronted with. There was no time for distractions—they had to act fast to combat the blaze and ensure everyone's safety.

Harry's mind was now focused on finding another water source. Amidst her frantic search, Pierre's muffled voice could be heard from inside the burning building, sounding like he was soothing someone or urging them to stay awake. Just as Harry braced herself to rush into the smoke-filled structure, she caught sight of Pierre emerging, dragging a limp body behind him.

Without hesitation, she sprinted towards Pierre, helping him pull the large man he was dragging behind him away from the engulfing flames and smoke. As they laid the man down, Harry recognized the unconscious figure as Reggie.

Pierre kneeled beside Reggie. "Stay back a bit, Harry," he instructed, his voice calm but urgent. Pierre had lost the towel that he had wrapped around his head. Harry saw steam rise off his hair and shoulders, showing how incredibly hot it was inside the reception area.

Harry watched on as Pierre gently shook Reggie's shoulder. "Reggie, can you hear me?" There was no response. Pierre then leaned close to Reggie's mouth, patiently looking, listening, and feeling for any sign of life.

"Reggie's breathing, but it's shallow," Pierre finally announced, his tone grave but controlled. He quickly felt Reggie's neck, his fingers pressing gently but firmly on the side. "I can feel a pulse, but it's weak."

Pierre then tilted Reggie's head back slightly and scanned Reggie's face and torso for any visible injuries, speaking as he did so. "We need to keep his airway clear. Harry, can you find something to prop under his shoulders? We need to keep him slightly raised to help with his breathing."

As Harry scurried to find a suitable cushion, Pierre continued his vigil over Reggie, constantly checking his breathing rhythm and pulse. His actions were methodical and precise, displaying the skills of a seasoned firefighter adept at handling such emergencies.

The tense air was thick with the heat of the blaze as Pierre braced himself to re-enter the building. He turned to Harry, about to instruct her on what to do next when suddenly, a deafening explosion erupted. Instinctively, they both ducked down, covering their heads with their arms as a brutal wave of heat and the force of the blast swept over them.

Pierre, his protective instincts kicking in, shouted to his wife, "*Dominique, ça va?*" His voice was laced with concern.

From behind a hedge, Dominique responded, her voice trembling but audible. "*Je vais bien, juste un peu secouée!*"

Harry's ears rang with the aftermath of the blast, muffling the sounds around her. She strained to hear as Pierre explained, "That probably is the gas bottles in the utility room, or maybe another gas source. Imagine if we arrive just a little late for Reggie. *Mon Dieu!*"

As they cautiously raised their heads, the sight before them was one of utter devastation. The building was now a raging inferno, its structure completely succumbing to the merciless flames. It was clear that any further attempts to check for survivors inside the building would prove futile.

Just then, Harry's phone buzzed with several notifications. Her hands, still trembling, fumbled as she checked the device. Amidst the chaos, an email subject line caught her eye:

Harry, it's urgent - read this as soon as you can!

For a moment, Harry was again torn between the immediate emergency and her desire to read the message. Her heart raced as she quickly scanned the contents of the email. The revelation it held was startling.

"Pierre, I have to go. There's something urgent I need to do. Can you handle things here with Reggie?"

"Go, Harry. We'll be okay. I can hear the fire trucks."

As Harry sprinted back towards the beach, the distant wail of sirens grew louder, signaling the imminent arrival of help. A wave of cool relief washed over her, knowing the fire would soon be under control.

Her mind, however, was singularly focused. The email she had just read made the puzzle pieces fall into place. Zoë's killer was out there, possibly mingling among the oblivious party-goers, unaware that Harry was on their trail. She quickened her pace, determination fueling her every step. The party's chaotic energy now served as a backdrop to her mission of bringing a killer to justice.

CHAPTER 28

THE ESCAPE

T he woman steered the speedboat skillfully across the calm sea, her heart pounding with fear and adrenaline. She had narrowly escaped, having managed to deceive everyone at the Hideaway. As the boat sliced through the water, she couldn't help but curse Zoë Kessler, the nosy reporter who would not stop asking questions. Until her arrival, everything had been proceeding smoothly.

She had envisioned a new life for herself here, a fresh start away from her complicated past. But Zoë's incessant snooping, her journalist's instinct to probe and question, had threatened to unravel everything. The woman frowned, recalling the questions that had started circulating about her. Was she really Thai? Why did she speak Thai with an accent? It was Zoë's prying that had alerted her staff, who then told Somchai about the American woman asking a lot of questions about her.

Now, under the guidance of the full moon, she navigated toward the mainland, her path illuminated by its silvery glow. Somchai knew this route well, having taken countless tourists to Surat Thani and occasionally meeting with the gang's cell there. Once in the city, her plan was to board a train to the Malaysian border. Her mind flickered to the fake passport she had acquired—a prudent investment from a skilled forger. It was her ticket to a new identity, a new life.

As the fleeing boat cut through the waves, she reminisced about her arrival in Bangkok a few years earlier, on the run from the FBI and private detectives. That was when she had decided to reinvent herself, to become a Thai citizen, leaving Samantha Chen, her old self, behind. But now, with her cover blown and her plans in jeopardy, she knew she had to disappear again. The risk of being caught was too high. Harry and her friends had come dangerously close to exposing her. With fearful determination, she focused on the journey ahead, ready to start again.

The woman's mind wandered back to when she first met Reggie. She had invested most of her resources into building the extravagant Hideaway, envisioning it as the perfect front for her more profitable island activities. It was more than just a retreat; it was a strategic façade for her shadowy dealings. Within a year, she had taken over a large chunk of the drug market in the Gulf of Thailand. It was her knowledge of Western tastes and her Asian appearance that did the trick. Foreigners trusted the quality of her products, and locals liked her. Those who didn't want to hand over their business to her were brutally persuaded to do so. Poison and arson were her tools of the trade.

Knowing that wealthy Americans were still looking for her, hoping to get their money back, she needed to stay in the shadows. She had required a frontman. Her initial encounter with Reggie had seemed like a stroke of luck. When he walked into the Hideaway two years earlier, she immediately recognized him for what he was—a conman, not as clever as she was, but a trickster nevertheless and a narcissist to boot. She had concocted a flimsy story about wanting to remain anonymous as the actual owner of the Hideaway, a tale she barely had to sell to Reggie. He latched onto the idea with greedy eagerness, relishing the opportunity to parade around the resort as the ostentatious, affluent owner-manager.

Sometimes, she mused, Reggie appeared to get lost in his fabricated persona, almost believing his own pretense of grandeur. But any semblance of sympathy she might have had for him evaporated without a trace. She harbored no remorse for knocking him unconscious and leaving him in the flaming office. In her calculated world, Reggie was nothing more than a convenient scapegoat—a puppet in her play. She had little time to organize her escape. Once the friendly constable had tried to impress her by telling her he was part of a sting operation at the Full Moon Party, she knew her days at the Hideaway were numbered.

Somchai envisioned the police piecing together a sad narrative of suicide, misled into believing Reggie had taken his own life over the Hideaway's entanglement with the drug cartel. It was the perfect cover-up, diverting attention away from her and cementing her escape. As she steered the boat, her thoughts were cold, focused solely on self-preservation and the new identity that awaited her beyond the Thai border. The Hideaway, Reggie, and her past life were just fading echoes in the night, left behind in the wake of her relentless pursuit of a new beginning.

As the boat motored further away from the shores of Koh Phangan, a wave of disappointment washed over the bitter woman. She reflected on the immense effort and cunning it had taken to establish the business and craft her new identity. Samantha had transformed herself into the affable Thai receptionist, Somchai, the indispensable right-hand girl to the manager, a persona that demanded her constant presence in the shadows, away from prying eyes. She had enjoyed that role. Because of her ethnicity and job title, people made immediate assumptions that she was of no importance and had no agency. It was the best disguise.

But this role had been her most challenging yet. Learning Thai, adopting a new culture, and navigating the treacherous waters of dealing with ruthless criminals had tested her in ways she hadn't imagined. But the allure of the lucrative business she had built kept her motivated. Selling drugs at the legendary Full Moon Party was her brainchild, a masterstroke in her enterprise.

The Full Moon Party, with its throngs of young, adventure-seeking revelers, provided the perfect cover for her activities. The partygoers, intoxicated and eager for new experiences, were an easy target. Drug sales skyrocketed, and the business flourished like never before. Even after the cartel in Surat Thani took its cut for its 'protection', the profits were immense.

As she navigated the boat under the moonlit sky, she couldn't help but lament the loss of her most profitable venture. All her hard work, the risks she took, the persona she painstakingly had built up—all were now slipping away like sand through her fingers. But the threat of being caught and recent events at the Hideaway had left her with no choice. She had to leave it all behind—her little empire on the island, her identity, her newfound wealth—all sacrificed for the sake of survival and the hope of starting anew elsewhere.

The night out at sea was cloaked in a tense stillness, broken only by the drone of the speedboat's engine and its spinning propeller slicing through the water. Somchai was lost in her reverie of past exploits and narrow escapes when an unfamiliar sound intruded upon her thoughts. At first, it was just a distant low frequency hum, almost imperceptible. But as it grew louder, her heart began to race, a sense of dread creeping over her. The sound was unmistakable now—another boat, and it was moving fast.

Her eyes scanned the dark waters, and soon enough, the ominous sight of flashing lights appeared on the horizon, the unmistakable silhouette of a powerful Coast Guard vessel. Hot panic surged through her veins, but she was not one to surrender easily. Gripping the throttle, she pushed the engine to its limit, her boat surging forward as it cut through the waves at a slightly higher speed.

The chase was on. Her small boat danced over the water, the engine roaring as she zigzagged in a desperate attempt to evade her pursuers. The full moon cast a silvery glow over the scene, creating a surreal, shimmering, watery backdrop to the high-speed pursuit.

From the powerful Coast Guard boat, a man's voice boomed over a megaphone, filling the night air with an authoritative command in English. "Samantha Chen, also known as Somchai Chen! This is the Coast Guard. You are under arrest. Cut your engine and surrender immediately. Do not attempt to flee. You will not escape. Compliance is your only option."

The man's words echoed across the water, a direct and non-negotiable demand. But Somchai was not ready to give in. Her mind raced as she calculated her next move, her hands steady on the wheel despite the turmoil she felt within. The pursuit intensified the roar of the engines of the pursuing boat, thundering in a relentless crescendo around her. Water sprayed in all directions as the boats maneuvered close to each other at breakneck speeds. Each turn of the wheel was a gamble between Somchai's freedom or capture.

Now, in the dead of night, with only the disinterested moon and the highly motivated Coast Guard as her companions, Samantha Chen, a woman who had evaded capture so many times, faced her most perilous escape yet. Then, through the din of the hectic chase, a familiar voice broke through, amplified and clear. It was Harry speaking through the megaphone.

"Samantha! Samantha Chen! Somchai! Please stop the boat. It's over. There's nowhere left to run. Every port has been alerted. They're all looking for you. You can't escape," Harry's voice pleaded.

Samantha's grip on the wheel tightened once again, her heart pounding in her chest. She felt that she was so close to escape.

"Think about it, Samantha!" Harry continued. "Don't you want the world to know about your genius, your ingenuity? If you disappear now, your story, your legacy, it all vanishes with you."

"Your work deserves recognition. I've read Zoë's magazine feature about you. The daughter of poor Chinese Cambodian immigrants who became a Californian socialite. You took from the rich. I understand why. Those spoiled brats didn't deserve their fortunes. Don't you want to share your story with the world?"

Samantha's mind raced. The idea of her life's work being acknowledged and admired struck a chord with her narcissistic outlook on life. She imagined herself on the cover of *Vanity Fair* or, even better, *Time* magazine. That would be the cherry on top. Was this her chance for infamy, for her story to be told? Was it time to stop running and let the world admire her ingenuity, her cunning?

As the minutes ticked by, her engine's roar began to wane, and Samantha's boat began to decelerate. She mulled over Harry's words. Perhaps there was truth in them. The world should know her story, recognize her brilliance, and marvel at the scale of her cons. A new kind of fame awaited her, not as a shadowy figure in the criminal underworld but as a mastermind whose cunning had captivated an entire island. She felt that she had nothing else to lose.

With a deep breath, she finally cut the engine, her boat coming to a gradual stop as it bobbed on the moonlit sea. She was ready to embrace this new chapter, to bask in the notoriety that her incredible life story would bring. As the Coast Guard closed in, Samantha Chen, the elusive con woman, prepared to reveal herself to the world.

Chapter 29

NEW DAY

Connor sat comfortably on the airy veranda of his picturesque Thai cottage on Koh Tao. The early morning sun cast a warm glow over the languid sea. He had been engrossed in reading an article on his cell phone detailing the astounding cons of Samantha Chen.

THE GREAT DECEPTION:

Unmasking the Californian Con Artist in Thailand

By Zoë Kessler & Henrietta Sinclair

Samantha Chen, once a familiar name in California's most elite circles, has now become infamous for weaving an intricate web of deception that spanned continents. Known for mingling with movie stars, tech moguls, and business tycoons, Chen's charm was as disarming as it was dangerous.

Her trail of cons began with a string of high-profile scams back in the States, where she convinced a Silicon Valley CEO's son to invest in a fabricated tech startup, siphoning off millions from the family's fortune. In another scheme, she persuaded the daughter of a Hollywood producer to funnel family funds into a non-existent film project, promising her an executive producer credit. These victims, driven by shame and fear of public humiliation, remained silent, allowing Chen to continue her crime spree unchecked.

Chen's scams were not the work of an amateur. She meticulously crafted the persona of an heiress with vast offshore wealth, convincing her victims that she could double or even triple their investments through her phantom ventures in Hong Kong and Shanghai. The money she stole funded an opulent lifestyle that only further cemented her image as a wealthy Asian socialite. For years, she navigated California's high society with ease, her true identity hidden beneath complex layers of lies and extravagance.

But as the saying goes, all good things must come to an end. When one of her victims—a New York-based venture capitalist—began to question the legitimacy of the returns on his investment, law enforcement agencies were alerted. The net of legal scrutiny tightened around Chen, with private investigators and police hot on her heels. As they closed in, Chen vanished without a trace, leaving behind bewildered victims and a trail of financial ruin.

Months later, she resurfaced, not as Samantha Chen, but as 'Somchai Chen', a seemingly affable Thai woman with a knack for hospitality. Under this new guise, she founded Mango Moon Hideaway, an upscale resort on Koh Phangan, which quickly became a sought-after destination for Western tourists in search of an authentic Thai experience.

Her transformation from Samantha to Somchai was nothing short of remarkable. Chen not only changed her name but also reinvented her entire identity. She immersed herself in Thai culture, mastered the language, and adopted the country's customs, effectively erasing her Californian past. To most visitors, she was an affable and helpful Thai receptionist. To the local staff, who spoke Thai, she explained that she was originally Cambodian.

But as recent events have shown, the truth has a way of surfacing. In a dramatic turn of events, a police sting operation at Mango Moon Hideaway led to Chen's arrest. Initially, authorities suspected Reginald Winthorpe, the official manager of the resort, to be the mastermind behind a drug distribution ring operating out of the Hideaway. Winthorpe, an American with a penchant for impersonating Australian MasterChef judge Matt Preston, was seen as the likely ringleader.

However, thanks to the courageous collaboration of several guests, the investigation took a sharp turn. It was revealed that the true architect of the criminal operation was none other than Chen herself—known to all as the 'manager's' factotum. Operating under the radar as 'Somchai', she had orchestrated a sophisticated money laundering scheme, using the resort as a front for her illegal activities.

As the police closed in on her, Chen made a desperate attempt to cover her tracks. She set fire to the main office of the Hideaway, hoping to destroy any physical evidence that could expose the full extent of her dealings, including secret bank accounts and records of her involvement in the distribution of drugs across the Gulf of Thailand. To make sure there were no witnesses, she left Winthorpe behind, unconscious after striking him on the head. The fire quickly spread, threatening to consume the entire building.

It was only due to the quick thinking and bravery of a French guest, Pierre Dubois, that Winthorpe was pulled from the flames just moments before a massive explosion destroyed the main building. Dubois' heroism not only saved a life but also preserved a vital witness.

Now in police custody, Samantha Chen faces a slew of charges, including fraud, money laundering, arson, and attempted murder. Thai authorities are considering extraditing her to the United States, where she will likely face additional charges related to her crimes there. As the investigation continues, it becomes clear that Chen's story is far from over.

This article marks the beginning of a series that will delve deeper into the murky dealings of Samantha Chen, the so-called 'Somchai'. Future articles will uncover the extent of her criminal network, the identities of her accomplices, and the shocking truth hidden beneath the surface of the seemingly idyllic Mango Moon Hideaway. Stay tuned as we unravel the web of deceit spun by one of the most cunning con artists of our time.

Setting the phone down on the rattan coffee table, Connor took a leisurely sip of his coffee and turned to Harry, who was seated beside him.

"So, did you write the second half?" Connor asked, his eyes curious.

Harry nodded, a thoughtful look on her face. "Yes, I did. I've been working with Zoë's editor and revising her articles. It's now turned into a complete series—an exposé of Samantha Chen's cons spanning from the US to Asia. It's so sad that Zoë was silenced because she almost had all the facts and evidence ready to publish. I believe she was days away from pulling out and going back to the States to write it all up."

Connor's expression turned serious. "When I accessed Zoë's cloud storage and started reading her work, I immediately knew you had to be informed. You needed to know exactly who you were dealing with."

Harry sighed, her gaze drifting towards the horizon. "If you hadn't sent me that article, we might never have caught Samantha. She would've been miles away by now, probably forging a new identity. She's like a social chameleon. Detective

Niran discovered that there was a snitch at the station, or not really a snitch but a blabbermouth."

"Really?"

"One of the constables who helped look for Sarah at the Hideaway fell for Somchai and invited her for drinks. He told her about the sting operation. He didn't know that she was the ringleader. That's why she started destroying the evidence."

Connor nodded, his eyes meeting hers. "It's incredible how she adapted and blended into so many lives, leaving chaos in her wake."

Harry looked back at the sea, the sun now a little higher in the sky. "Well, thanks to your help, her days of deception are over. Now, her story will be told, but on our terms."

The two sat in contemplative silence, savoring their coffee as the peaceful morning on Koh Tao unfolded around them.

"How did you manage to catch Somchai? Or should I say, Samantha?"

Harry, recalling the night's events, began to explain. "It was Pierre who gave me the idea. Earlier that evening, he mentioned seeing one of the local detectives at the party. When I read your email, I didn't know what else to do, so I ran back to the beach to look for him."

She paused, sipping her coffee. "The fire scared everyone, and with the music off, it was somewhat easier to search through the crowd. It took a a couple of minutes, but I finally found the detective."

Connor nodded, hanging on every word.

"I told him everything I knew about Somchai's true identity," Harry continued. "It was almost like he had been expecting something like this to happen. He immediately got on the radio to communicate with his team."

Harry's eyes lit up as she recounted the next part. "It turned out they had a whole police team monitoring the Full Moon Party. One of the officers reported seeing a speedboat with a single woman on board leaving the Hideaway not long before. We didn't waste any time after that."

Connor's expression was a mix of admiration and disbelief. "So, it was all about being in the right place at the right time and a bit of quick thinking."

"Exactly. Samantha might have slipped through our fingers if it weren't for Pierre's observation and the detective's quick response."

The sun continued to rise, and the bright light that fell on the gardens surrounding the cottage contrasted with the cool shade of the veranda.

"The detective asked me to accompany him on the Coast Guard boat. He thought he might need a woman fluent in English to convince Samantha to stop."

Harry leaned back, remembering the tense moments on the water. "As we were catching up to her, he filled me in on their plan. They were actually conducting a sting operation that night. They knew about the drug sales at the Hideaway's Full Moon Parties but hadn't pinpointed the organizer. They suspected it was Reggie, the manager." Harry's expression turned serious. "Their plan was to nab the dealers first, then move on to Reggie. That's why there were undercover officers at the party."

Connor listened intently, piecing together the events. "So, Somchai must have sensed the heat closing in, which is why she set up Reggie as the fall guy. Oh my God! I sound just like a New York gangster."

"Yeah, you do." Harry agreed. "Perhaps I am a bad influence on you." She laughed.

"Anyway, if it hadn't been for Pierre finding Reggie and rescuing him from that burning office, he might not have made it. He was totally unaware of what Somchai was plotting behind his back."

"How did you catch her?"

"When we were chasing after her boat, I was thinking of how to convince her to stop. I decided to appeal to her narcissistic traits—I assumed that, like most con artists, she must have a grandiose personality, believing that she is better and smarter than everyone else. I told her it would be a shame if the world didn't hear her story. It must have struck a chord because she stopped the boat."

Connor's curiosity was evident. "Did Samantha say anything to you on the way back to shore?"

Harry nodded, recalling the encounter. "She asked me which magazines were going to feature her story. She talked about *Vanity Fair* and *Time*. I think she already imagined herself on the covers. When I told her I wasn't sure, she became very cold, almost arrogant. She didn't act like she had done anything wrong. As if being caught was just an inconvenient setback."

"Sounds like you judged it correctly. She might be a sociopathic narcissist. No empathy for others."

"Exactly," Harry agreed. "To her, we're all just pawns in her game."

She then recounted more of her conversation with Samantha. "She asked how I had found out about her. She thought she had disposed of all the evidence when she threw Zoë's laptop into the sea. I told her about the cloud storage, and she was furious with herself for overlooking that detail."

"I asked her if she was the one who tried to kill you by swapping the chips in your packet for shrimp-flavored ones. She denied it, but there was this vile smirk on her face. She's obviously trying to limit the number of charges against her."

Connor, concerned, asked, "What's going to happen to her now?"

"The detective said she'll be tried in Thailand first for drug dealing, arson, and the attempted murder of Reggie," Harry explained. "And then she'll be extradited to the US to face the fraud charges. She's got a long road ahead."

Harry shook her head in disbelief as she recalled Samantha's final words.

"As we were parting, she said she'll sell the rights to her story to a streaming movie channel one day and make millions. Even though she had just been arrested, she was already plotting her next move. It was eerie how positive she was, already scheming her next scam."

Connor sighed, his expression turning somber. "I'm just grateful you and Euclid found me when you did. When my throat started to close up, and I couldn't find my EpiPen... it was the worst moment of my life."

Harry reached over and gently touched his arm. "I'm grateful too, Connor. The mere thought of what might have happened if we hadn't found you in time... it's terrifying."

Deep in thought, Connor reflected on the convoluted situation he had found himself in. "Samantha really was a clever criminal. Proving she tried to kill me would be incredibly difficult. Even if the police found her fingerprints in my hut, she was part of the staff, so her prints could be argued to be there legitimately. What about Zoë's murder? Will they be able to bring Somchai to justice for that?"

Harry sighed, feeling the gravity of the situation. "I spoke to Detective Niran about my suspicion that Somchai poisoned Zoë. It wasn't just a gut feeling—there was something more. I told him about a piece of paper that Reggie had on his clipboard, an order for rodent poison. It got me thinking about strychnine. It's not something you can easily get your hands on, but it is used in industrial settings, like for keeping rodents out of a big resort."

"Strychnine? Did they find it in Zoë's system?"

"They did," Harry confirmed. "They found exactly that. But you have to look specifically for it because it doesn't show up in a regular drug test. I think Somchai handed Zoë a strychnine-laced drink during the foam party—do you remember how she and Reggie were serving everyone these elaborate cocktails? Who could refuse? Then she watched Zoë suffocate and die under the cover of foam. It was Somchai who first suggested to the police that Zoë might have died of secondary drowning. Once that idea was planted, the police seemed to dismiss the case. They didn't even look for another explanation."

Connor frowned, absorbing the new information. "But what about Reggie? Was he truly innocent in all of this?"

Harry paused, uncertainty creeping into her voice. "I don't know for sure. Reggie can attest that there was strychnine missing from the storage closet, which is why he had to make that extra order for rat poison. Reggie was adamant something was wrong, but Somchai pretended nothing was missing. The thing is, I'm not sure how much Reggie really knew about her drug dealings. Maybe he was so engrossed in playing the manager that he chose to turn a blind eye to what was actually going on around him."

Connor nodded, understanding the murky waters they were navigating. "It's hard to say. Zoë deserves justice, but these cases are so complex, especially when you're dealing with someone as manipulative and calculating as Somchai."

Their conversation trailed off as they both sat, lost in thought, contemplating the difficulties the police faced in proving a case of murder, along with the elusive nature of justice.

"And have you had any news from Euclid and Sarah?" Connor asked.

Harry retrieved her phone and showed Connor the email from Euclid.

Harry,

I'm writing to let you know not to worry about me and Sarah. It turns out Sarah got herself accidentally involved with a local drug cartel and was held by them for a few days. Fortunately, one of the gang members was actually an undercover policeman. Sarah and I spent the night of the Full Moon Party in a police cell incognito, with only the friendly detective in the know about our whereabouts. In the morning, he dropped us off at the harbor, and we took the first ferry to the mainland. We're flying back to Seoul tonight.

We are so sorry we didn't get to say goodbye in person, but the detective insisted on us keeping a low profile for the safety of his undercover officer. Please say goodbye to Connor for us. Harry, we now consider you a friend for life. We hope you'll visit us in Seoul before you head back to the US. And good luck with your search for closure regarding your parents' accident. This isn't goodbye, but rather a 'see you very soon'. Sarah sends all her love. She'll need some therapy and support when we get home, but she's strong. I'm sure she'll be fine after a while.

Best,

Euclid

Connor looked up from the phone, his expression a mix of relief and concern. "I'm so glad they're safe. It sounds like they've been through quite the ordeal."

"Yes, they have. But they're resilient. I'll definitely try to visit them in Seoul. It's amazing how situations like these can bring people together and forge such strong bonds."

Connor's expression was one of somber introspection as he revisited the chain of events in his mind. "I have to admit, for a while, I was convinced Reggie was behind Zoë's murder."

"I felt the same way. Remember when we overheard Reggie on his cell phone when we broke into Zoë's hut? He was speaking German to someone in the middle of the night. That really made me suspicious."

"Yes, that's exactly the moment that solidified my suspicions about him."

"Well, I asked him about it. It turns out that wasn't what we thought. I found out that Reggie's parents are originally from East Germany. They sought political asylum in the US back in the seventies. Reggie was born in the US and grew up bilingual, speaking English and German fluently.

"That night on the phone, he was actually talking to his octogenarian father, who was updating him about his mother's hip replacement surgery. He was outside because he was so worried about her and couldn't sleep. You know the time difference between the US and Thailand is almost 12 hours. That's why he was on the phone in the middle of the night."

Connor let out a small laugh, a mix of relief and disbelief. "That makes a lot more sense now. I guess it's a lesson not to jump to conclusions based on incomplete information."

"I suppose we all learned not to jump to conclusions. I was so taken by the charming Somchai that I trusted everything she told me. I can see how people fell for her cons. I also saw her as 'just' a receptionist and didn't even consider her as a possible suspect."

"Talking about stereotyping people," Connor said, giving Harry a reproachful look, "I spoke to Grove Manning the other day. You made me worried when you said he disappeared from social media, so I located him. He is a really nice chap. He stopped posting after Zoë's death because he was too heartbroken. The two of them were just starting to hit it off and were planning to travel together to Bali for a romantic getaway."

"Oh, that's terrible. I feel awful for making assumptions about him. To be honest, at some stage, I thought it might have been him that Zoë was investigating."

As Connor finished his coffee, he turned his attention to Harry. "What are your plans now? Are you going to stay on Koh Tao for a bit longer?"

Harry glanced out towards the sea, then back at Connor. "I was actually hoping you might let me stay here for a couple of weeks."

"Be my guest. I've rented this cottage for a month. I've got a work project to focus on, and I need to stay put until it's done."

"That suits me perfectly," Harry replied, a hint of relief in her voice. "I need to catch up on my writing, too. I've neglected my travel blog for far too long." She checked a note on her phone and added, "Plus, I need to find someone named 'Crazy Olga'. She might hold the key to uncovering the truth about my parents' death."

Connor looked intrigued. "That sounds like quite a task. What are your plans for today, then?"

Harry stretched out luxuriously on the rattan armchair, finishing her coffee. "Today? Today, I plan on doing absolutely nothing. Just take in the beauty of this place and relax."

Harry smiled as she took in the breathtaking views of Koh Tao. The lush green of the coconut palm trees was beautifully complemented by the turquoise waters. The sounds of jungle creatures living their innocent jungle life softly echoed in the background. Today would be a much-needed day of respite for Harry—one spent in paradise.

WHISPERS OF LOTUS VILLA

I f you enjoyed *Moonlit Secrets*, get *Whispers of Lotus Villa* from any major online bookstore!

Preface: The Glow

I move stealthily through the jungle while the beam of my torch slices through the thick midnight air. The moon is a dull whisper behind the clouds, leaving me to rely on my instincts and the faint ambient light. Around me, the night is alive with sound, including the haunting call of an owl and the rhythmic chirping of a nightjar. They are my only companions.

Clasping my phone, I squint closely at the screen where an online map shows a solitary pin—my destination. The path before me is narrow, almost swallowed by the wild embrace of the trees and bushes. I tread carefully, mindful of every snapped twig and crunched leaf beneath my boots.

After thirty minutes stretched into an eternity, the looming silhouette of an abandoned village emerges. It's a ghostly sight of the remnants of lives once lived in peace but now surrendered back to Nature. A tiny flicker of light catches my eye in the heart of this abandoned desolation. I have reached the meeting point.

My heart pounds against my ribcage like a relentless drum beating out the chaotic rhythm of my anxiety. I remind myself of the rules: stay clear and don't touch anything. The risk I run is monumental, and the consequences of a misstep are catastrophic.

I silently inch closer to the light. This isn't just a simple, one-off transaction; it's the culmination of years of meticulous planning, constituting a pivotal step in a grander scheme. It's my legacy.

I take a deep breath to steady my nerves and step into the pool of flickering light. My wavering shadow stretches out behind me, merging with the darkness I've left behind. I have reached the point of no return.

I step inside the dilapidated building. Before me stand two young Cambodian men, their presence here clearly for mutual support and protection. Without wasting time on inane pleasantries, I cut straight to the chase.

"Where is it?"

Without uttering a word, they lead me to the remnants of a radiotherapy machine. I listen intently as they explain its history. A Dutch medical charity had once tried to bring hope to this forsaken village by building a specialized cancer clinic. The clinic was a beacon of hope for those unable to afford the long journey to the nearest city. But a volcanic eruption had destroyed almost everything, leaving the clinic abandoned and forgotten. The Dutch charity was dissolved and disbanded, leaving behind this piece of equipment now standing before me.

"When was the last time anyone asked about this place?" I inquire, scrutinizing their faces for any hint of deception.

"Since the volcano, five years ago. People have forgotten about this place," one of them replies.

I ponder their response. They could be lying, but it doesn't matter. The contents of this machine are what I'm after. The money I'm offering should ensure their silence. For a moment, I consider the finality of a pair of well-placed bullets to ensure their permanent silence, but I reluctantly dismiss the thought. Anyway, I am sure they have already told someone else about this meeting. It's safer to just pay them and vanish.

I hand over the backpack, watching as they greedily unzip it and start counting the cash—$100,000. To them, it's a fortune; to me, it's a mere pittance, a small price to pay for what I'm about to acquire.

As the men count the money, my mind drifts to the treasure hidden that lies deep within the machine. The thought of its fluorescent glow, the key to my ambitious plan, makes it difficult to suppress my smile of satisfaction. My plan is coming together wonderfully, and soon, the world will witness its fruition.

Chapter 1 Catching Up

Amaya, her curly black hair framing her face and piercing black eyes scanning the shelves, strolled through the aisles of a quaint Thai supermarket on Charoen Krung Road in Bangkok. The market was alive with the vibrant hues and aromas of fresh produce—spiky rambutans with their soft, juicy white flesh, purple-skinned mangosteens revealing a sweet, tangy surprise, and unmistakable durians, their unique scent permeating the air. Some dragon fruit, with their striking pink and green exteriors, nestled beside a small pyramid of ripe, golden mangoes.

In the vegetable section, fresh Thai basil filled the air with its unmistakable fragrance as it blended with the lemony scent of lemongrass stalks. Bunches of crisp *bok choy* and green morning glory were neatly arranged in rows alongside tiny but fiery bird's eye chilies and plump eggplants.

As Amaya carefully selected her ingredients, she was preoccupied with the dinner she had planned for tonight. Harry, her dear friend, was due to arrive for a stay of a few weeks. She was also bringing Connor along, a young man she had grown close to in Koh Phangan. Amaya had decided to prepare something special for them—self-constructed Thai Spring Rolls. She imagined the fun they would have, rolling their own spring rolls, customizing them to their own taste. She thought it would be a meal that encouraged conversation and participation and would be perfect for catching up with Harry and getting to know Connor better.

For dessert, Amaya decided that a fruit-based dish would be refreshing. She settled on Mango Sticky Rice, a classic Thai dessert. It was simple but delightful—sweet, ripe mangoes served with sticky rice, drizzled with creamy coconut milk, and sprinkled with toasted mung beans for a contrasting, peppery crunch.

With her shopping bags full of all the necessary ingredients, Amaya made her way to the checkout. Her heart fluttered with excitement and anticipation, not just for the reunion with Harry but also for the chance to get to know Connor. Tonight, she hoped that her home would be filled with the warmth of friendship, the air rich with the aromas of Thai cooking, and the echoes of shared laughter and stories.

As she waited in line, she looked at her cell phone, hoping to see a message from her friend, an American artist whose studio was next to hers, but there was nothing. He hadn't replied to her messages sent the day before, and she was starting to worry, but then she also knew that she often kept her cell phone away when she worked on her art, especially when she felt inspired.

He's probably busy in the studio, Amaya reassured herself and decided not to send any more texts. *I'll stop by to check on him when I can.*

As she walked home, she breathed in the comfortably warm air typical of early autumn in Bangkok. Charoen Krung Road, one of the city's oldest streets, was lined with an array of architecture that spoke of the kingdom's connection to Europe during the Victorian era. The buildings, a mix of old and new, were predominantly informed by European styles, reflecting the time when Western influence shaped the city's urban landscape. Among these buildings, the colonial-style edifices still stood out with their distinctive features, including grand façades, tall, narrow windows with shutters, and ornate balconies decked with filigreed ironwork. These structures, once symbols of European power, were now seamlessly woven into the fabric of modern Bangkok.

As she walked on, Amaya admired the lush greenery that functionally decorated the urban environment. The tops of the tall, slender palm trees swayed gently in the breeze, their fronds rustling softly like tissue paper wrapping a precious gift. Interspersed among palm trees were the smooth trunks of mighty hardwood trees, their branches spread wide to provide welcome shade to the pedestrians below. Gnarled bougainvillea vines bursting with splashes of vibrant pink and purple climbed along walls and fences and added vivid color to the scene.

The street was alive with the typical hustle and bustle of any Bangkok thoroughfare. Every fifty meters or so, street vendors sold aromatic Thai dishes, and small side-walk cafes served fresh homemade meals. The occasional tuk-tuk zipped by, the passengers holding on tightly to chromed grab handles and plastic shopping bags. The sounds of the city – a metropolitan blend of fleeting conversation, polite laughter, and the hum of traffic – created a lively yet comforting ambiance.

As Amaya approached her building, her attention was drawn to the backs of two young people seated on a bench nearby, engaged in a lively conversation. The girl, sporting an underlayer hairstyle with light green strands cheekily peeking from behind her blond hair, exuded a carefree aura. Her sun-kissed skin, athletic build, and tall stature suggested an independent life filled with adventure and outdoor activities.

Beside her sat a young man, his age hovering around late twenties or early thirties. Some of his dark, curly hair flowed from under a stylish sports beanie, complementing his short, thick beard. His olive-tanned skin made his bright smile even more striking, giving him a clean, approachable look.

Amaya's street observations were cut short. The girl turned around. Instantly, her face lit up with recognition.

"Amaya!" she exclaimed, her voice ringing with joy. "It's so good to see you!"

Amaya smiled broadly, her heart swelling with happiness. "Harry! I'm so happy you're here! I love the green hair. It suits you!"

"Thank you! It was time for a change."

The two friends shared a warm, affectionate hug. Harry stepped back, turning to the young man beside her.

"And this is Connor," she said, gesturing towards him. "Thanks so much for letting him come along."

Connor stepped forward, extending his hand toward Amaya with a friendly smile. "Hi, Amaya. Really do appreciate you hosting us. It's great to meet you."

Amaya shook his hand, feeling the sincerity of his words. "Of course, Connor. It's a pleasure to meet you, too. Well. Welcome to Bangkok!"

The happy exchange set a cheerful tone and promised that they would all have a memorable time together. As the pair gathered their backpacks and headed towards the building, Amaya felt a rising sense of excitement for the days to come.

Chapter 2 The Letter

I stare out the window at the lotus pond and the lush garden beyond. The heavy scent of rain and flowers lingers, the tranquility of the scene mocking the turmoil roiling within me. In my hand, I clutch a letter. The name on the envelope makes my blood boil. How did they find this address?

Reluctantly, I slip on gloves and goggles before opening it—always cautious, always prepared. As I unfold the note inside, my stomach tightens. The words, scrawled in an untidy hand, spin a pathetic tale of illness and accusation.

Good Day!

First of all, I want to thank you for your generosity in supporting my art. I have some bad news. I have not been feeling very well recently and have been in and out of hospital. Local doctors are puzzled. It seems I may have to go back to the US to seek treatment.

As much as I appreciate your generosity in commissioning my talent, I feel I need to be compensated for my health issues; if not, I plan to expose your dealings. As you can see, it was not too difficult for me to figure out your real name and address.

My account is the same as in the past.

Kind regards,

BJ

I slam my hand onto the antique desk, the resounding crack startling the mynah bird in its cage by the window. It squawks, mimicking the curse that bursts from my lips. The echo of its voice only fuels my anger. How dare this little weasel threaten me? I've spent years perfecting this plan. A perfect plot to rid the world of its parasites.

My thoughts churn, the artist's words clawing at my composure. I'm sure the idiot did not follow the protocol I set for him. How else did he get ill?

I ball the letter in my gloved hand, glaring at the wood-paneled walls that once soothed me. This setback is trivial. I won't let it derail everything. The fundraiser looms large in my mind—a stage set for the rich and privileged to meet poetic justice. Their yachts, their obscene homes, their gilded lives—it all sickens me. The money they hoard should flow, lifting the masses they exploit.

I glance at the letter again, my lips curling into a grim smile. He won't stop me. None of them will. I've worked too hard to bring my vision to fruition.

Leaving the study, I step into the atrium of the Lotus Villa, the air cool and heavy with the scent of jasmine. Around me, the sculptures sit, each one a masterpiece in more ways than one. My fingers brush over a carving of Vishnu, marveling at the intricate details that hide its true purpose. Next, I pick up a delicate Cambodian Apsara dancer. The cool metal feels like reassurance in my hands.

Finally, I approach the centerpiece: a Laughing Buddha. Its joyous expression conceals the lethal secret buried within. My fingers trace its rounded belly, a sense of satisfaction settling over me. The design is perfect—subtle and slow, a ticking clock only I can hear. Months, maybe a year, before it takes effect. I might not be around to witness the fallout, but that doesn't matter. My legacy will be unstoppable, a force reshaping the world long after I'm gone.

I step back, surveying the collection with a mixture of pride and grim determination. The plan is in motion, unstoppable now. The wealthy will pay for their greed. And if a few innocents fall along the way? That's just collateral damage—a small price for a better world. I need to get rid of the weakest link first, though, before he derails my life's work.

Get *Whispers of Lotus Villa* from any major online bookstore!

Harry Sinclair's Koh Phangan's Recipes

CRAB STIR-FRIED WITH YELLOW CURRY

Greetings, fellow wanderlusters and food enthusiasts! It's Harry Sinclair here, sharing yet another delectable discovery from my culinary adventures around the globe. This time, I'm taking you on a journey to the enchanting island of Koh Phangan in Thailand, where I experienced an unforgettable evening and an equally unforgettable dish: Poo Phad Phong Karee, or Crab Stir-Fried with Yellow Curry.

Poo Phad Phong Karee Recipe

Ingredients:

1 large crab, cleaned and cut into pieces

2 tablespoons vegetable oil

1 onion, thinly sliced

3 cloves garlic, minced

1 red bell pepper, sliced

1 yellow bell pepper, sliced

2 tablespoons yellow curry powder

1 tablespoon fish sauce

2 tablespoons soy sauce

1 tablespoon oyster sauce

1 tablespoon sugar

1/2 cup chicken or vegetable broth

1/2 cup coconut milk

2 eggs, lightly beaten

2 green onions, chopped

Fresh cilantro for garnish

Instructions:

1. Prepare the Crab: Begin by cleaning the crab thoroughly and cutting it into manageable pieces. This can be a bit tricky, so don't hesitate to ask your fishmonger to do this for you.

2. Heat the Oil: In a large wok or skillet, heat the vegetable oil over medium-high heat. Once hot, add the sliced onion and minced garlic. Sauté until the onion becomes translucent and the garlic is fragrant.

3. Add the Bell Peppers: Toss in the red and yellow bell peppers, stirring frequently until they start to soften. This should take about 3-4 minutes.

4. Incorporate the Spices: Sprinkle in the yellow curry powder, ensuring that it evenly coats the vegetables. Stir-fry for another 2 minutes to release the flavors of the curry.

5. Flavor the Dish: Add the fish sauce, soy sauce, oyster sauce, and sugar to the wok. Mix well to combine all the ingredients, creating a harmonious blend of flavors.

6. Simmer the Crab: Add the crab pieces to the wok, followed by the chicken or vegetable broth. Cover and let it simmer for about 5 minutes, allowing the crab to absorb the fragrant spices.

7. Create the Sauce: Pour in the coconut milk, stirring gently to mix it with the curry and broth. Let the mixture simmer for another 3 minutes.

8. Finish with Eggs: Slowly pour the beaten eggs into the wok, stirring continuously to create a silky, thickened sauce. The eggs will cook almost instantly, adding richness to the dish.

9. Garnish and Serve: Finally, add the chopped green onions and give the dish one last stir. Garnish with fresh cilantro and serve hot with steamed jasmine rice.

CRAB TOM YUM SOUP

As I stepped off the boat onto the sun-kissed shores of Koh Phangan, I was immediately enveloped by the vibrant energy of this island paradise. Known for its full moon parties and serene beaches, Koh Phangan also boasts an incredible culinary landscape. It was here, in a quaint beachfront hut, that I had my first taste of **Tom Yum with Crab**—an iconic Thai soup that balances the fiery, the tart, and the savory in a harmonious medley that dances on your palate. This experience not only deepened my love for Thai food but also inspired me to bring a piece of Koh Phangan to you.

Ingredients:

2 large crabs, cleaned and cut into pieces

4 cups of water

2 stalks lemongrass, cut into 1-inch pieces and smashed

6 kaffir lime leaves, torn into pieces

4 slices galangal, thinly sliced

6 Thai bird chilies, smashed (adjust to taste)

200g straw mushrooms, halved

3 tablespoons fish sauce

2 tablespoons lime juice (or to taste)

2 teaspoons sugar

1 cup cherry tomatoes, halved

1 small bunch of cilantro, roughly chopped

2 spring onions, chopped into 1-inch pieces

1 tablespoon chili paste in oil (optional, for extra heat and color)

Instructions:

1. Prepare the Soup Base: In a large pot, bring the water to a boil. Add the lemongrass, kaffir lime leaves, and galangal. Simmer for 5 minutes to release the flavors.

2. Add the Crab: Place the crab pieces into the boiling broth. Reduce the heat and simmer gently until the crab is cooked through, about 10 minutes.

3. Flavor the Soup: Stir in the straw mushrooms, cherry tomatoes, and smashed bird chilies. Continue to simmer for an additional 5 minutes.

4. Season the Soup: Add the fish sauce, lime juice, sugar, and chili paste in oil (if using). Adjust the seasoning to balance the sour, salty, and spicy flavors according to your preference.

5. Garnish and Serve: Just before serving, add the chopped spring onions and cilantro for freshness.

6. Enjoy: Serve hot, ensuring each bowl gets a generous portion of crab and a balance of mushrooms and tomatoes.

Harry's Tips:

Fresh Ingredients: Make sure your ingredients are fresh, especially the crab, for the best flavor.

Adjust Spiciness: The heat level can be adjusted by increasing or reducing the number of bird chilies.

Serving: This soup is perfect with a side of steamed jasmine rice to soak up the flavorful broth.

Thai cuisine is a testament to the country's ethos of balance and variety, reflected in dishes that are as diverse as its landscapes. Whether you're a seasoned chef or a curious novice, trying your hand at this recipe can transport you to the warm, tropical waters of Koh Phangan without leaving your kitchen. So dive into this dish, and let the vibrant flavors bring the spirit of Thai islands right to your home, one sumptuous bowl at a time.

THAI CUCUMBER SALAD

Hello, fellow adventurers and culinary explorers! Harry Sinclair here, bringing you another delightful entry from my food-filled travels. This time, we're diving into the vibrant world of Thai side dishes – the unsung heroes that elevate every meal with their bold flavors and fresh ingredients. While Thai main courses often get the spotlight, it's the side dishes that truly complete the experience.

In this post, I'll introduce you to some quintessential Thai side dishes: Thai Cucumber Salad, Spicy Green Papaya Salad, and Stir-Fried Morning Glory. I'll also share recipes for each, along with tips on how to substitute ingredients that might be hard to find in your local grocery store. Let's get started!

Thai Cucumber Salad (Yam Tua Kiew)

This refreshing salad is a perfect complement to spicy Thai dishes. It's light, crisp, and bursting with tangy flavors.

Ingredients:

1 large cucumber, thinly sliced

1 small red onion, thinly sliced

2 tablespoons sugar

2 tablespoons rice vinegar (or white vinegar)

1 tablespoon fish sauce (or soy sauce for a vegetarian option)

1 small red chili, finely chopped (optional)

Fresh cilantro for garnish

Instructions:

1. Prepare the Cucumber and Onion: In a large bowl, combine the sliced cucumber and red onion.

2. Make the Dressing: In a small bowl, whisk together the sugar, rice vinegar, fish sauce, and chopped red chili.

3. Combine: Pour the dressing over the cucumber and onion, tossing to combine.

4. Garnish: Garnish with fresh cilantro before serving.

Substitute Tip: If you can't find rice vinegar, white vinegar works just fine. For those who prefer a milder flavor, you can skip the chili.

SPICY GREEN PAPAYA SALAD

This iconic Thai salad is known for its spicy, tangy, and slightly sweet flavor profile. It's a must-try for any Thai food enthusiast.

Ingredients:

1 small green papaya, peeled and shredded

2 cloves garlic, minced

2-3 Thai chilies, finely chopped (adjust to taste)

2 tablespoons fish sauce

1 tablespoon lime juice

1 tablespoon sugar

1/2 cup cherry tomatoes, halved

1/4 cup roasted peanuts

Fresh basil or cilantro for garnish

Instructions:

1. Shred the Papaya: Use a grater or a mandoline to shred the green papaya into thin strips.

2. Prepare the Dressing: In a mortar and pestle, pound the garlic and chilies until they form a paste. Add the fish sauce, lime juice, and sugar, mixing until the sugar dissolves.

3. Combine: In a large bowl, combine the shredded papaya, cherry tomatoes, and roasted peanuts. Pour the dressing over the salad and toss well.

4. Garnish: Garnish with fresh basil or cilantro before serving.

Substitute Tip: If green papaya is unavailable, try using shredded green apples or zucchini for a similar texture and flavor.

STIR-FRIED MORNING GLORY

This simple yet flavorful dish is a staple in Thai cuisine, known for its garlicky and savory taste.

Ingredients:

1 bunch of morning glory (water spinach), cut into 2-inch pieces

3 cloves garlic, minced

1-2 Thai chilies, chopped

2 tablespoons oyster sauce

1 tablespoon soy sauce

1 teaspoon sugar

2 tablespoons vegetable oil

Instructions:

1. Prepare the Morning Glory: Rinse the morning glory thoroughly and cut into 2-inch pieces.

2. Stir-Fry the Aromatics: In a large wok, heat the vegetable oil over medium-high heat. Add the minced garlic and chopped chilies, stir-frying until fragrant.

3. Add the Greens: Add the morning glory to the wok, stirring constantly.

4. Season: Add the oyster sauce, soy sauce, and sugar, continuing to stir-fry until the greens are tender but still crisp.

5. Serve: Serve hot as a side dish.

Substitute Tip: If you can't find morning glory, spinach or kale can be used as substitutes. Just adjust the cooking time as needed since these greens cook faster.

Bringing Thai Flavors to Your Table

These side dishes not only add vibrant flavors to your meal but also showcase the diversity and richness of Thai cuisine. Each dish is a testament to the balance of sweet, sour, salty, and spicy flavors that Thai food is famous for.

So, the next time you're looking to spice up your meal, try incorporating one (or all!) of these Thai side dishes. They're sure to impress your family and friends and transport you straight to the bustling markets and serene beaches of Thailand.

THAI GREEN CURRY

Today, I want to take you on a flavorful journey through the world of Thai curries. As a travel blogger and a devoted foodie, I've had the pleasure of tasting some of the most exquisite dishes across the globe, but there's something uniquely enchanting about Thai curries that keeps me coming back for more. Let's delve into what makes Thai curries so special and how they differ from their Indian counterparts. And, of course, I'll share my favorite recipe for the vibrant and delicious Thai Green Curry, or Kaeng Khiao Wan.

The Essence of Thai Curries

Thai curries are a symphony of flavors, combining aromatic herbs, spices, and fresh ingredients to create a harmonious balance of sweet, salty, sour, and spicy. Unlike Indian curries, which often have a thicker, creamier consistency due to the use of dairy products like yogurt or cream, Thai curries are typically lighter and brothier. The use of coconut milk in Thai cuisine imparts a rich, silky texture and a subtle sweetness that perfectly complements the heat of the chilies.

Key Differences Between Thai and Indian Curries

1. Base Ingredients: Thai curries often use fresh ingredients like lemongrass, galangal, kaffir lime leaves, and Thai basil, which contribute to their distinctive flavor profile. Indian curries, on the other hand, rely heavily on dried spices such as cumin, coriander, turmeric, and garam masala.

2. Cooking Techniques: In Thai cuisine, curry pastes are usually made fresh and then fried in oil to release their aromas before adding coconut milk and other ingredients. Indian curries typically involve roasting and grinding spices or using pre-ground spice mixes to create a complex, layered flavor.

3. Heat Levels: While both Thai and Indian curries can be quite spicy, Thai curries often use fresh chilies, including the fiery bird's eye chili, to bring the heat. Indian curries may use a variety of dried chilies and chili powders, resulting in a different kind of spiciness.

Recipe for Thai Green Curry (Kaeng Khiao Wan)

Now, let's get cooking! Here's a simple yet delicious recipe for Thai Green Curry that you can easily recreate at home.

Ingredients:

1 lb (450g) chicken breast or tofu, cut into bite-sized pieces

1-2 tbsp green curry paste (adjust to your spice preference)

1 can (14 oz/400 ml) coconut milk

1 cup chicken or vegetable broth

1-2 tbsp fish sauce (or soy sauce for a vegetarian option)

1 tbsp palm sugar or brown sugar

2-3 kaffir lime leaves, torn into pieces

1-2 Thai bird's eye chilies, sliced (optional for extra heat)

1 small eggplant, chopped

1 red bell pepper, sliced

1 cup baby corn, halved

1 cup bamboo shoots

1 cup fresh Thai basil leaves

Juice of 1 lime

Instructions:

1. Heat a large pot or wok over medium heat. Add a small amount of coconut milk and the green curry paste. Stir well and cook until the paste is fragrant and slightly darkened.

2. Add the chicken or tofu pieces to the pot, stirring to coat them in the curry paste. Cook for a few minutes until the chicken is no longer pink on the outside.

3. Pour in the remaining coconut milk and the chicken or vegetable broth. Bring to a gentle simmer.

4. Add the fish sauce, palm sugar, kaffir lime leaves, and sliced chilies (if using). Stir well to combine.

5. Add the eggplant, red bell pepper, baby corn, and bamboo shoots. Simmer for about 10-15 minutes, or until the vegetables are tender and the chicken is fully cooked.

6. Remove from heat and stir in the fresh Thai basil leaves and lime juice.

7. Serve your Thai Green Curry hot, over steamed jasmine rice, and enjoy the explosion of flavors!

Happy cooking and bon appétit!

GREEN CURRY PASTE

In my previous post, we explored the vibrant world of Thai Green Curry, a dish that tantalizes the taste buds with its harmonious blend of flavors. Today, I'm excited to share with you the secret behind the magic: the Green Curry Paste. Making your own curry paste at home ensures the freshest flavors and allows you to tailor the heat and spice to your liking.

Homemade Green Curry Paste

Ingredients:

5-7 green Thai bird's eye chilies (or substitute with serrano peppers for milder heat)

1-2 jalapeño peppers (for added green color and a bit more heat)

1 lemongrass stalk, trimmed and thinly sliced (substitute with 1 tbsp lemon zest if unavailable)

1-inch piece of galangal, peeled and sliced (substitute with 1-inch piece of ginger)

4-5 cloves of garlic, peeled

2 shallots, peeled and roughly chopped (substitute with 1 small yellow onion)

1 tsp kaffir lime zest (substitute with regular lime zest)

2-3 kaffir lime leaves, finely chopped (optional, substitute with extra lime zest if unavailable)

1/2 cup fresh cilantro leaves and stems

1/2 cup fresh Thai basil leaves (substitute with Italian basil if unavailable)

1 tsp ground coriander

1 tsp ground cumin

1/2 tsp white pepper

1 tsp salt

2 tbsp fish sauce (substitute with soy sauce for a vegetarian option)

1 tbsp shrimp paste (optional, omit for vegetarian)

1-2 tbsp water or vegetable oil (for blending)

Instructions:

1. In a food processor or blender, combine all the ingredients except the water/vegetable oil.

2. Blend until smooth, adding water or vegetable oil as needed to achieve a thick, paste-like consistency.

3. Taste and adjust the seasoning, adding more salt or fish sauce if needed.

4. Store the paste in an airtight container in the refrigerator for up to 1 week, or freeze it in ice cube trays for longer storage.

Substitutes for Hard-to-Find Ingredients:

1. Thai Bird's Eye Chilies: These can be quite spicy and hard to find. Serrano peppers or jalapeños make good substitutes, though they are milder. For more heat, you can add a pinch of cayenne pepper.

2. Lemongrass: If you can't find fresh lemongrass, use lemon zest and a bit of lemon juice to mimic its citrusy flavor. Lemongrass paste, available in tubes at some grocery stores, is also a convenient alternative.

3. Galangal: This unique root has a slightly peppery, citrusy flavor. Ginger is the best substitute, though the flavor will be slightly different.

4. Kaffir Lime Leaves/Zest: Kaffir lime leaves impart a unique, fragrant citrus flavor. If you can't find them, use extra lime zest and a small amount of lime juice.

5. Thai Basil: Italian basil can be used as a substitute, though Thai basil has a more anise-like flavor. Adding a small amount of fennel seeds can help mimic this taste.

Making your own green curry paste not only elevates your cooking but also gives you a deeper appreciation for the intricate flavors of Thai cuisine. Don't let the unavailability of certain ingredients deter you. With these substitutes, you can still enjoy a delicious and authentic-tasting Thai Green Curry right in your own kitchen.

I hope you enjoy crafting and cooking with your homemade green curry paste. Stay tuned for more recipes and travel tales as we continue our culinary adventures together!

THAI-INSPIRED BREAKFAST BOW

Hello, lovely readers! It's Harry Sinclair here, sharing a delightful twist on your morning routine that blends the freshness of Thai fruits with the creaminess of Greek yogurt, all topped off with a crunchy, homemade granola. This Thai-inspired Greek yogurt breakfast bowl is not only a vibrant start to your day but also packed with nutrients that will keep you energized and satisfied.

Thai-Inspired Greek Yogurt Breakfast Bowl

Ingredients:

1 cup Greek yogurt

1/2 cup mixed Thai fruits (such as mango, dragon fruit, and pineapple), chopped

1 tablespoon honey or to taste

1 tablespoon chia seeds

2 tablespoons mixed nuts (such as cashews and almonds), roughly chopped

2 tablespoons fresh coconut shavings

Instructions:

1. Prepare the Fruit: Peel and chop your selected Thai fruits into bite-sized pieces.

2. Assemble the Bowl: In a serving bowl, spoon the Greek yogurt. Drizzle with honey and mix slightly to sweeten the yogurt evenly.

3. Add Toppings: Scatter the chopped fruits over the yogurt. Sprinkle the chia seeds, chopped nuts, and coconut shavings evenly over the top.

4. Garnish and Serve: Add a few mint leaves for a fresh touch. Dive in and enjoy the fusion of creamy, crunchy, and tropical flavors in each spoonful!

HOMEMADE TROPICAL GRANOLA

Creating your own granola can be wonderfully satisfying, and it allows you to control the ingredients to suit your health preferences. Here's how to make a simple, healthy granola that's perfect for pairing with your yogurt bowl.

Ingredients:

2 cups old-fashioned oats

1/2 cup mixed nuts (almonds, walnuts, cashews), chopped

1/4 cup seeds (sunflower or pumpkin seeds)

1/4 cup unsweetened coconut flakes

1/4 cup dried fruits (raisins, cranberries)

1/4 cup honey or maple syrup

1/4 cup coconut oil, melted

1 teaspoon vanilla extract

1/2 teaspoon cinnamon

Instructions:

1. Preheat the Oven: Set your oven to 300°F (150°C) and line a baking sheet with parchment paper.

2. Mix Dry Ingredients: In a large bowl, combine oats, chopped nuts, seeds, and coconut flakes.

3. Combine Wet Ingredients: In another bowl, whisk together the melted coconut oil, honey (or maple syrup), vanilla extract, cinnamon, and salt.

4. Combine and Spread: Pour the wet ingredients over the dry ingredients and stir until everything is well coated. Spread the mixture evenly onto the prepared baking sheet.

5. Bake: Bake for about 25-30 minutes, or until the granola is golden brown, stirring halfway through to ensure even baking.

6. Cool and Store: Allow the granola to cool completely on the baking sheet. It will crisp up as it cools. Once cool, stir in the dried fruits. Store the granola in an airtight container at room temperature for up to 2 weeks.

Serving Suggestion:

Combine this homemade granola with the Greek yogurt bowl for a delightful crunch, or enjoy it with a splash of milk or on top of smoothies for added texture and flavor.

This Thai-inspired Greek yogurt breakfast bowl paired with homemade granola offers a delicious and nutritious start to your day, blending exotic flavors with wholesome ingredients. Enjoy the freshness of each bite and the energy it brings to your morning!

SIAM SUNRAY & BANGKOK BREEZE

Hello, fellow travelers and cocktail enthusiasts!

As we journey through the vibrant flavors of Thailand, I couldn't resist sharing a couple of my favorite Thai-inspired cocktails. Perfect for summer or any time you want to transport your taste buds to an exotic paradise, these drinks are sure to impress. Let's dive into the recipes for the refreshing 'Siam Sunray' and the invigorating 'Bangkok Breeze'.

Siam Sunray: A Tropical Delight

The 'Siam Sunray' is a delightful blend of vodka, coconut milk, and a touch of chili, capturing the essence of Thailand in a glass. It's the perfect balance of creamy, spicy, and refreshing.

Ingredients:

2 oz vodka

1 oz coconut milk

1 oz fresh lime juice

1 oz simple syrup

1 small red chili, thinly sliced (remove seeds for less heat)

Ice

Lime wedge and chili slice for garnish

Instructions:

1. In a shaker, combine the vodka, coconut milk, fresh lime juice, simple syrup, and a few slices of red chili.

2. Fill the shaker with ice and shake vigorously until well chilled.

3. Strain the mixture into a glass filled with ice.

4. Garnish with a lime wedge and a slice of chili.

5. Serve and enjoy the tropical kick!

Bangkok Breeze: A Refreshing Escape

The 'Bangkok Breeze' is a concoction of gin, lemongrass, and kaffir lime leaves. This aromatic cocktail is both refreshing and complex, perfect for sipping on a warm evening.

Ingredients:

2 oz gin

1 oz lemongrass syrup (recipe below)

1 oz fresh lime juice

2-3 kaffir lime leaves, torn

Soda water

Ice

Lemongrass stalk and lime wheel for garnish

Lemongrass Syrup:

1 cup water

1 cup sugar

2 stalks lemongrass, chopped

Instructions for Lemongrass Syrup:

1. In a saucepan, combine water, sugar, and chopped lemongrass.

2. Bring to a boil, then reduce heat and let simmer for 10 minutes.

3. Remove from heat and let cool completely. Strain and store in the refrigerator.

Instructions for Bangkok Breeze:

1. In a shaker, combine the gin, lemongrass syrup, fresh lime juice, and torn kaffir lime leaves.

2. Fill the shaker with ice and shake well to mix and chill.

3. Strain the mixture into a glass filled with ice.

4. Top up with soda water and gently stir.

5. Garnish with a lemongrass stalk and a lime wheel.

6. Serve and enjoy the refreshing escape!

STIR-FRIED PORK WITH THAI BASIL AND CHILIES

Hello again, culinary adventurers! It's Harry Sinclair here, ready to guide you through another flavorful journey with one of Thailand's most beloved street foods: Pad Krapow Moo. This quick and spicy stir-fry dish combines succulent pork with fragrant Thai basil and fiery chilies, all topped with a fried egg if you like it the traditional way. Whether you're cooking a quick dinner or craving something deeply satisfying, this dish promises to deliver bold flavors in every bite.

Ingredients:

1 pound ground pork

2 tablespoons vegetable oil

5 cloves garlic, minced

5-8 Thai chilies, finely sliced (adjust based on your heat preference)

1 red bell pepper, thinly sliced (optional for added color and sweetness)

2 tablespoons oyster sauce

1 tablespoon soy sauce

1 tablespoon fish sauce

1 teaspoon sugar

1 cup Thai basil leaves (holy basil, if available)

Fried eggs (one per serving, optional)

Instructions:

1. Prepare the ingredients:

Peel and mince the garlic and slice the chilies. If using a bell pepper, slice it thinly. Pluck the basil leaves from their stems.

2. Cook the Pork:

Heat the vegetable oil in a wok or large frying pan over high heat. Add the minced garlic and chilies, sautéing until aromatic. Be careful not to burn the garlic.

Add the ground pork, breaking it up with your spatula. Fry until the pork is fully cooked and starting to brown.

3. Season the Dish:

Add the oyster sauce, soy sauce, fish sauce, and sugar to the pork. Stir well to combine all the ingredients and coat the pork evenly. If you've added bell pepper, toss it in now and cook for an additional minute.

4. Add the Basil:

Reduce the heat to medium-high and add the Thai basil leaves. Stir-fry for about 30 seconds or until the basil is wilted and fragrant. The heat should be high enough to allow the basil to release its flavors without wilting too much.

5. Serve:

Serve the Pad Krapow Moo immediately, ideally with a fried egg on top of each serving. This dish goes perfectly with steamed jasmine rice.

Serving Suggestions:

Pad Krapow Moo is traditionally served over rice with a fried egg whose runny yolk adds a creamy texture to the spicy, flavorful pork and basil.

Harry's Tips:

Basil Substitutes: If Thai basil is hard to find, you can use regular sweet basil. The flavor will be different, but it will still be delicious.

Adjusting the Heat: The number of chilies can be adjusted according to your spice tolerance. Start with fewer and add more as needed.

HARRY'S GUIDE TO RICE

Hello, culinary explorers! It's Harry Sinclair here, bringing you a guide that will transform how you think about and cook one of the most essential staples in kitchens worldwide: rice. Rice is incredibly versatile and can be paired with a myriad of dishes, but getting it right can be the difference between a good meal and a great one. Here's my comprehensive guide on how to cook rice perfectly every time and how to choose the right type of rice for different dishes.

Cooking Perfect Rice

1. Basmati Rice

Best for: Indian and Pakistani cuisines, pilafs

How to Cook: Rinse the rice under cold water until the water runs clear. This removes excess starch and prevents the rice from becoming gummy. For every cup of rice, use 1.5 cups of water. Bring to a boil, then cover and reduce to a simmer for 15-18 minutes. Let it sit, covered, for 5 minutes after turning off the heat, then fluff with a fork.

2. Jasmine Rice

Best for: Thai and Southeast Asian dishes

How to Cook: Rinse the rice until the water is clear. Use a 1:1 ratio of rice to water. Bring the water to a boil, add the rice, stir once, and cover. Reduce the heat to low and simmer for 18 minutes. Remove from heat and let it sit, covered, for 10 minutes before fluffing.

3. Sushi Rice

Best for: Sushi and Japanese dishes

How to Cook: Wash the rice in several changes of water until the water is clear. Drain well. Use a 1:1.2 ratio of rice to water. After bringing to a boil, cover and simmer on low for 18 minutes. Remove from the heat and let it sit for 10 minutes. Season with sushi vinegar while still warm.

4. Arborio Rice

Best for: Risotto and Italian dishes

How to Cook: Arborio rice is typically not rinsed, as the excess starch contributes to the creaminess of the risotto. Toast the rice in oil or butter until translucent before adding broth gradually, stirring continuously until the rice is al dente.

5. Long-Grain White Rice

Best for: General use in a variety of global dishes

How to Cook: Rinse the rice until the water is clear. Use a 1:2 ratio of rice to water. Bring to a boil, then cover, reduce the heat to low, and simmer for 20 minutes. Remove from heat and let it sit, covered, for another 10 minutes.

6. Brown Rice

Best for: Health-conscious meals with robust, nutty flavors

How to Cook: Brown rice requires more water due to its fibrous bran coating. Use a 1:2.5 ratio of rice to water. Bring to a boil, then cover, reduce the heat to low, and simmer for 45 minutes. Remove from heat and let it sit, covered, for 10 minutes.

Pairing Rice with Dishes

Basmati Rice: Perfect for soaking up the rich spices in curries and balanced well with the robust flavors of biryani.

Jasmine Rice: Ideal with Thai curries, grilled fish or chicken, and stir-fried vegetables, where its subtle sweetness complements spicy and bold flavors.

Sushi Rice: Must be paired with vinegar and fresh fish for sushi or served alongside Japanese curry.

Arborio Rice: Essential for creamy risottos or used in Italian rice salads.

Long-Grain White Rice: A versatile choice that works well in Latin American dishes, similar to Gallo Pinto or West African Jollof rice.

Brown Rice: Great with grilled vegetables and lean proteins or as a base for hearty salads due to its chewy texture and nutty flavor.

With these tips, you'll be able to choose and cook your rice perfectly, enhancing both its flavor and compatibility with various dishes. Remember, rice is not just a side dish but a crucial component that can elevate your meals.

THAI-STYLE OMELET WITH JASMINE RICE

Hello from my kitchen to yours! It's Harry, ready to whisk you away to the vibrant flavors of Thailand with a simple yet delicious dish: Kai Jeow, a Thai-style omelet. This fluffy and slightly crispy omelet is a staple in Thai cuisine. It's quick and easy!

Ingredients:

3 large eggs

1 tablespoon fish sauce

1 tablespoon soy sauce

1 teaspoon sugar

2 green onions, chopped

1 small bunch of fresh cilantro, chopped (optional)

2 tablespoons vegetable oil

Jasmine rice, cooked and hot for serving

Instructions:

1. Prepare the Rice:

Begin by cooking jasmine rice according to package instructions. You'll want it hot and ready to serve with the omelet.

2. Mix the ingredients:

In a mixing bowl, crack the eggs and add fish sauce, soy sauce, and sugar. Beat the mixture with a fork or whisk until everything is well combined and slightly frothy. Stir in the chopped green onions and cilantro (if using).

3. Cook the Omelet:

Heat the vegetable oil in a non-stick frying pan or wok over medium-high heat. Once the oil is hot, pour in the egg mixture. The egg should sizzle as it hits the pan.

Let the eggs cook undisturbed for about 1 minute or until the edges start to lift from the pan and are golden brown.

Gently lift the edges of the omelet and tilt the pan to let the uncooked egg flow to the edges. Continue cooking until most of the egg is set, but the top is slightly runny.

4. Flip the Omelet:

Carefully flip the omelet over to cook the other side, about 30 seconds to 1 minute, until it is fully set and golden. Some people prefer their Kai Jeow a little crispy, so feel free to cook it a bit longer if desired.

5. Serve:

Slide the omelet onto a plate and serve it hot over a bed of jasmine rice.

Serving Suggestions:

Kai Jeow can be enjoyed as it is or with a side of Thai chili sauce (sriracha) for an extra kick. It's commonly eaten any time of day and can be a quick breakfast, a light lunch, or a comforting dinner.

Harry's Tips:

Customizing Your Omelet: Feel free to add minced pork, diced tomatoes, or thinly sliced onions into the egg mixture before cooking for added texture and flavor.

Achieving the Perfect Texture: The key to a great Kai Jeow is the heat of your oil; it should be hot enough so that the egg puffs up slightly when it cooks, giving you those delicious crispy edges.

THAI LEMON TEA

Hello, dear readers! Harry Sinclair here, your enthusiastic guide to the flavors of the world. Today, we're exploring the vibrant tea culture of Thailand, with a special focus on a refreshing favorite, Cha Manao, or Thai lemon tea. Whether you're wandering through a bustling Thai market or sitting back in your own home, Thai teas offer a delightful experience, each sip brimming with tradition and taste.

Cha Manao: Thai Lemon Tea

Cha Manao, which translates to "lemon tea" in Thai, is a popular drink in Thailand, known for its refreshing and invigorating qualities. It combines the bold flavors of black tea with the bright zest of fresh lemon, often sweetened, to create a perfectly balanced beverage. Here's how you can make it at home:

Ingredients:

4 cups of water

4-5 black tea bags (or about 4 tablespoons of loose black tea)

Juice of 2 large lemons

¼ cup of sugar, or to taste

Ice cubes

Fresh mint leaves or lemon slices for garnish (optional)

Instructions:

1. Brew the Tea: Bring water to a boil in a pot. Add the tea bags or loose tea (ideally in a tea infuser) and let them steep for about 5 minutes.

2. Sweeten: Remove the tea bags or infuser. While the tea is still warm, dissolve the sugar into it. Adjust the sweetness according to your preference.

3. Add Lemon: Once the tea has cooled slightly, stir in the fresh lemon juice. Mixing the lemon juice while the tea is not too hot preserves its vibrant flavor.

4. Chill: Transfer the tea to a pitcher and let it cool to room temperature. Then refrigerate until cold.

5. Serve: Fill glasses with ice, pour the chilled lemon tea over, and garnish with mint leaves or a slice of lemon.

ABOUT THE AUTHOR

Sabina O. is the pseudonym of Sabina Ostrowska, the author behind the bestselling *New Life in Andalusia* series. Enjoying life among the sunny olive groves of southern Spain, Sabina crafts her narratives with a vivid sense of place. *Moonlit Secrets* is the second installment in her culinary cozy mystery series where she invites readers on armchair adventures that span the globe. So, pour yourself a glass of your favorite beverage and delve into a world of secrets.

To receive the news of the latest releases and giveaways in the Harry Sinclair Cozy Travel Mystery series, sign up with your email via her website.

www.sabinaostrowska.com

Sign up here!

Or follow her on social media:

Facebook @sabinawriter

Instagram @sabina.author

TikTok @sabina.author

ALSO BY

A Harry Sinclair Cozy Travel Mystery series so far:

Shadows of Serenity

Moonlit Secrets

Whispers of Lotus Villa

Sabina's Humorous Non-fiction Series:

The Crinkle Crankle Wall: Our First Year in Andalusia

A Hoopoe on the Nispero Tree: Our Andalusian Adventure Continues

Olive Leaf Tea: Time to Settle

ACKNOWLEDGEMENTS

Creating a book is like building a puzzle—it takes many pieces to form a complete picture. This cozy mystery, the second in Harry Sinclair's adventures, came together with the help of an incredible group of people who brought their unique contributions to the table.

First, my heartfelt thanks to Denver Murphy, my editor. Denver, your expertise and knack for storytelling were like a compass, keeping this book on course and guiding Harry Sinclair's world to vivid life. Your insights have been pivotal, and I'm deeply grateful for your guidance.

To my beta readers and reviewers: your thoughtful feedback and keen observations were like the missing pieces that completed the puzzle. A special shoutout to Teri Kellum, Lisa Zinn Christensen, Linda Ann Foster, and Mac Cochenour for your time, enthusiasm, and belief in this story. You kept me motivated and inspired with every chapter.

To my husband, Robert Ryan—your tireless support and sharp eye were like the glue holding everything together. Thank you for your patience during the final edits, encouragement, and for believing in this story as much as I do.

I also want to acknowledge the wonderful reader communities who have supported this series from its early days. To the **Cozy Mystery Reader Tribe**, **Cozy Mystery Village**, and **Cozy Mystery Party**, your enthusiasm and love for this genre have been a powerful force behind my writing. To all the readers within these groups, thank you for cheering me on and sharing your excitement—it means more than you know.

Lastly, to every reader who picks up this book: you're the final piece of this puzzle. Your curiosity and passion for cozy mysteries are what make this journey worthwhile. Thank you for joining Harry Sinclair on his latest adventure.

PHOTO CREDITS

www.ingramcontent.com/pod-product-compliance
Lightning Source LLC
LaVergne TN
LVHW041503170726
843492LV00005B/1356

9788409670864